THE ONLY WITNESS

Before there was the Phantom Menace, there was . . .

STAR WARS®

JEDI APPRENTICE

STAR WARS®

JEDI APPRENTICE SPECIAL EDITION
#1 Deceptions

JEDI APPRENTICE

The Only Witness

Jude Watson

SCHOLASTIC INC.

New York Toronto London Auckland Sydney
Mexico City New Delhi Hong Kong Buenos Aires

No part of this publication may be reproduced in whole or in part, or stored in a retrieval system or transmitted in any form or by any means, electronic, mechanical, photocopying, recording, or otherwise, without written permission of the publisher. For information regarding permission, write to Scholastic Inc., Attention: Permissions Department, 555 Broadway, New York, NY 10012.

ISBN 0-439-13936-8

Cover art by Cliff Nielsen.

12 11 10 9 8 7 6 5 4 3 2 1   2 3 4 5 6 7/0

Printed in the U.S.A.
First Scholastic printing, February 2002

THE ONLY WITNESS

Jedi Master Qui-Gon Jinn sighed deeply as he strode down the hall. The Council felt he had been inactive for too long, and he knew it. They had been patient as he mourned the death of his dear friend Tahl. And now they were waiting for him to decide he was ready to resume his active life as a Jedi.

Except he wasn't. And he was not sure he ever would be.

Qui-Gon turned a corner, heading for the Council room. The Council had summoned him, but hadn't explained why. Perhaps they had grown tired of waiting. Perhaps they were going to send him on a mission anyway.

Maybe it is for the best, Qui-Gon thought, trying to make himself believe it. He'd been attempting to convince himself of so many things lately, though he did not often succeed. *And at least it will be good for Obi-Wan.*

Qui-Gon's Padawan walked noiselessly beside him, his face a mask of perfect calm. Qui-Gon knew what lurked underneath. He could feel the tension growing between him and his apprentice. He sensed that Obi-Wan wanted to speak, and yet he was uncharacteristically silent.

Though Qui-Gon and Obi-Wan had never been far apart over the last few months, in many ways Qui-Gon had deserted his apprentice. He wished he could say something to reassure Obi-Wan. Soothing speeches used to come so easily. But Jedi wisdom felt somehow hollow to him now. He would not offer the boy empty words.

Pausing outside the Council room, Obi-Wan turned to his Master. Qui-Gon saw he was about to speak, but before he could say anything the Council room doors hissed open.

Only three of the twelve Council seats were filled. Qui-Gon was not surprised to see so few members present. He greeted his old friends and stood before them in the familiar circle.

Yoda, Mace Windu, and Plo Koon thanked the Jedi team for coming. Their eyes passed briefly over Obi-Wan, then rested on Qui-Gon. They were obviously concerned.

Qui-Gon could feel the Council members looking deep inside him, trying to determine if sending him on a mission was the right decision. He was surprised to find that he could not hold their gaze. Rather than lifting his burden of sorrow, their caring made him painfully aware of the weight he was bearing.

Looking past the seated Masters to the Coruscant skyline, Qui-Gon tried to settle his feelings. He wondered yet again why he could not let this flood of emotion flow through him. He had been taught to do just that by great teachers — some now seated before him — and it had always worked. Yet it did not work now.

Obi-Wan shifted his feet, and Qui-Gon realized that the silence had gone on for too long.

"We've received a request from Senator Crote of Frego," Mace Windu began at last. "He has asked for Jedi assistance in transporting a witness to Coruscant to testify before the Senate."

Qui-Gon nodded. Protecting important witnesses was routine for the Jedi. As he'd suspected, this first mission would be a simple assignment — something easy. A distraction. That was why there were only three members of the Council present.

"A simple task it is not," Yoda said, as if in answer to Qui-Gon's thoughts. "There is much danger on Frego."

Mace Windu continued to study Qui-Gon's face. "We would not send you if we did not think you were ready. Do you feel ready, Qui-Gon?"

Qui-Gon did not know. He had no desire to leave the Temple, or even his simple rooms. But it would not be fair to Obi-Wan to live in seclusion forever.

"I am ready," Qui-Gon replied, more firmly than he believed.

Qui-Gon could feel Obi-Wan's relief. It rushed from him like a breath that had been held for a long time and finally released. The Council members, too, seemed to relax upon hearing Qui-Gon's words. They stopped searching his thoughts. They had the answer they wanted. Qui-Gon hoped he had made the right decision.

"As Yoda said, the situation is complicated," Plo Koon said. "We've asked Jocasta Nu to give you all of the information you need before you depart." He gestured toward the Temple archives.

"Go now you must," Yoda added gravely.

"We fear the danger for the witness is growing. The sooner you get to Frego, the better," Mace said, dismissing Qui-Gon and Obi-Wan with a wave of his hand. "May the Force be with you."

Qui-Gon nodded and walked slowly out of the

circular room, followed by Obi-Wan. Even after hearing the Masters' cautionary words, he felt sure that the mission would be simple to complete . . . as long as his spirit didn't fail him.

Jocasta Nu was a thin, wispy Jedi with long graying hair that she wore in a tight bun. She stood up from her work table the moment the Jedi entered the room. The picture of efficiency, she gathered her materials and gestured toward another, larger table, asking Qui-Gon and Obi-Wan to take a seat.

"I understand that time is of the essence," Jocasta said. She did not bother with introductions. It did not matter. Qui-Gon had encountered the Temple archivist before, and surely Obi-Wan knew who she was. She briefed many Jedi teams before they went out on important missions.

In the past Qui-Gon had preferred to use other sources to get his information. He had grown used to working with Tahl, and hadn't met with Jocasta that often since he took Obi-Wan as an apprentice four years ago.

"The witness is Lena Cobral." Jocasta showed them a holo image of a slight young woman with dark hair twisted into an elaborate bun. "She is the widowed wife of Rutin Cobral."

The image of the young woman vanished and

a man appeared in her place. He was young, fairly tall, with short brown hair and a relaxed smile. "Rutin was recently killed, and his murderer is still at large."

"Is that unusual?" Qui-Gon asked. "I thought Frego was a planet ruled by criminals."

Jocasta looked slightly annoyed at the interruption, but continued. "The Cobral family is the largest power on Frego. They are in charge of a crime ring that has successfully controlled the government for twenty years. Rutin's father died a few years ago, of natural causes. It was widely believed that Rutin was being groomed to take over, although he has two brothers who are older than he is. Solan is the oldest and the new leader of the Cobral."

A shorter, stockier version of Rutin appeared on the screen. Besides his brother's height, Solan also lacked his thick head of hair and genuine smile. He was nearly bald and his scowl looked permanent.

"Solan is well known on his planet, widely feared and respected. He gets what he needs through threats, violence, and influence."

Now that Jocasta was through imparting information, she was prepared to answer Qui-Gon's question.

"It is not unusual for murders to go uninvestigated on Frego. But it is unusual for a favored member of the Cobral family to be killed, particularly without vengeance."

Though Qui-Gon's expression did not change, he felt a fresh wave of grief wash through him. He longed more than ever for Tahl — for her cynicism, her quick mind, and her habit of dispensing information in a way that naturally led Qui-Gon's thoughts in the proper direction.

Qui-Gon reminded himself that theirs was a relationship that had taken years to develop. And that the connection he had with Tahl was one he would never have with the Temple archivist. Or anyone else, probably.

"Lena married into the Cobral family three years ago," Jocasta went on. "There was a rumor that Rutin no longer wanted to be involved in his family's dealings. Although he could not easily divorce himself from the crime business, Senator Crote has told us that Rutin was prepared to testify before the Senate against his family. He wanted to put an end to the crime ring altogether. Not long after Rutin agreed to testify, he was killed." Jocasta took a breath, but did not allow more than a second to pass before going on.

"Last night we received a secret communication from Lena. Senator Crote did as well. She has decided to take up her husband's cause and testify against the Cobral herself." Jocasta pushed several documents on a datapad across the table toward the Jedi. "Everything you need is here."

Qui-Gon stood and took the datapad. "Thank you," he said curtly. "We may be contacting you if we need further assistance."

"Of course," Jocasta nodded. "May the Force be with you."

Qui-Gon nodded blankly in return. How could he trust that the Force would be with him? Where had it been when he'd needed it the most? He and Tahl had pledged their love for each other. But nothing — not that love, not the Jedi, not the Force — had been able to save her.

It did not take long for Qui-Gon and Obi-Wan to gather supplies for the short journey. Soon they were stepping onto the freighter that would take them to Frego.

Distracted and exhausted, Qui-Gon was anxious to retire to his quarters as soon as they were on board. He was about to say as much to Obi-Wan when his Padawan spoke.

"Master, I know that these last few months have been hard on you." Obi-Wan reached out a hand toward Qui-Gon's shoulder but let it drop, barely brushing his Master's brown sleeve. "And I . . . well, I can't help remembering what you told me when Bant was missing in the Temple. You said that the darkest time is the time when it is most important that you follow the Jedi Code. If you let your emotions fl —"

"Thank you, Obi-Wan," Qui-Gon cut him off. "You have learned well what I've taught you. One day you will make a fine Jedi Master." He turned and made his way quickly toward his quarters. He could sense the boy behind him, standing, bewildered.

Qui-Gon knew his apprentice was only trying to make him feel better. But he could not bear to listen to the wisdom that was now failing him. He simply wanted to be alone.

CHAPTER 2

Obi-Wan stood silently, watching the planet Frego grow larger on the freighter's viewscreen. Qui-Gon had not emerged from his quarters during the journey. Obi-Wan was not sure if he should disturb him, even now that they were drawing close to their destination. He desperately wanted to give Qui-Gon the same comfort his Master had given him so many times. But the more he tried, the further Qui-Gon retreated. The gulf between them seemed to be growing wider, and Obi-Wan was at a loss. How could he span the distance alone?

"That must be Frego."

Qui-Gon's voice surprised Obi-Wan and filled him with relief. He would not have to disturb his Master's solitude after all.

"And that glowing spot must be the capitol city of Rian," Qui-Gon continued.

Obi-Wan could tell that Qui-Gon was still sad

and distracted. It was almost like standing beside a ghost. But at least he was speaking. He
was making an effort.

As they exited the craft, Obi-Wan felt on edge.
It was up to him to focus on this mission. He
could not depend on his Master in his emotion-
ally wounded state.

Obi-Wan did not think the Cobral family had
been alerted to their arrival, but a planet ruled by
criminals was always a dangerous place. He half
expected to see dark dealings and black market
bargains right in the freighter hangar, but there
was only one person present as the Jedi disem-
barked — and she looked at them without interest. Obi-Wan relaxed a little, until the freighter
captain slid down the ramp toward him.

"I'll be taking off as soon as possible, if that's
okay," he said nervously. "I don't want to spend
any more time here than is absolutely necessary, with the Cobral airways tax and all."

Obi-Wan nodded. Though he did not know
exactly what the pilot was referring to, he could
tell it was not pleasant, and most likely not le-
gal. He thanked the captain for their safe passage and watched him slip back inside his craft.

As soon as the ship's door shut, the lone
woman in the hangar approached the Jedi.

"I trust you had a pleasant journey from . . ."
she paused.

"Coruscant," Obi-Wan finished for her. "Are you Lena?"

"No," the woman said, lowering her hood to reveal closely cut hair and a youthful face. "I am Mica, but I will take you to Lena now." Mica glanced around the hangar once more.

She's nervous, Obi-Wan thought. He drew a deep breath and concentrated on the Force. But he did not sense danger, only Mica's fear.

"Follow behind me, but not too close. If I am approached I will pretend not to know you." Mica's eyes were large and dark and she turned them on Qui-Gon and Obi-Wan in turn, waiting for each to nod in agreement.

"We will do as you ask," Obi-Wan assured her.

Raising her hood, Mica started out of the hangar at a brisk pace.

Obi-Wan enjoyed being introduced to a new planet on foot. Qui-Gon had taught him that the slower pace was best for observation, and there was much to observe in Rian. None of it was what Obi-Wan had expected.

The streets were clean; the footpaths were filled with Fregans carrying colorful bundles and walking unhurriedly together. Just a short distance from the municipal hangar, stalls lined the paths. Food vendors sold heaps of fresh fruits and vegetables, meats, and grains, shouting out prices and greeting regulars. Farther into the open market more vendors sold household goods and even crafts. Everywhere people seemed happy and relaxed.

In the heart of the market the crowd was so dense and there was so much to see that Obi-Wan nearly lost sight of Mica. But whenever he looked up he saw Qui-Gon's eyes trained on the gray peak of Mica's hood. He did not seem to be taking in the surroundings as he normally would. His thoughts were clearly elsewhere.

Obi-Wan would have liked to discuss his observations with his Master. Wasn't it unusual that a planet controlled by criminals would have such a seemingly happy populace? But he was quite sure Qui-Gon wasn't thinking about the Fregans, so he kept quiet.

At last the market stalls ended and the crowd thinned. After following Mica through a maze of dark but clean alleys, the woman stopped and beckoned the Jedi toward her. When they drew close Mica punched a control pad and a large warehouse door groaned open to reveal a huge room filled with abandoned equipment.

"We're here," Mica said, waving the Jedi in first and taking a last look up and down the alley before shutting the door. "I am the only one who knows where Lena is hiding. Besides you. It is important that you are never followed to this spot."

"Of course." Obi-Wan nodded.

At the top of several flights of durasteel stairs, the yawning spaces and hulking machinery gave way to a more hospitable living space. Standing with her back to the entrance among several mismatched but comfortable-looking couches was the woman Obi-Wan had seen on Jocasta Nu's holoscreen. Lena Cobral.

Mica cleared her throat to announce their arrival. Lena turned.

"You've made it," she said, bringing her hands together and offering both of them to Qui-Gon and then Obi-Wan, and finally embracing Mica. "I'm so pleased. Was your journey very difficult?"

"It passed quickly," Qui-Gon told her before introducing himself and Obi-Wan.

Obi-Wan was glad that Qui-Gon had emerged again from silence, for he was not entirely sure he would have been able to manage the conversation so easily.

Lena Cobral had been attractive on the holoscreen, but in person she was stunning. Her long dark hair spilled over her shoulders, framing her face and dark eyes like Mica's. She was only a few years older than Obi-Wan, which surprised him. Like the Fregans in the street, her demeanor was relaxed. She greeted the Jedi as if they were old friends or honored guests at a party, not political escorts.

"Please sit," Lena said, guiding the Jedi to the chairs. "You need refreshment. Perhaps some Kopi tea?"

Before the Jedi could protest Lena was pouring a warm dark liquid into cups. It looked slightly orange and tasted delicious.

"My cousin Mica brings me everything now that I am in hiding." Lena smiled at the silent Mica. "She brought me this tea yesterday. And today she has brought you to me as well." Lena turned her infectious smile on the Jedi; Obi-Wan found that it was nearly impossible not to smile back.

"She is too good to me." Lena's upbeat voice gave no clue that there was any real threat. "She insists on staying with me without any thought of the danger to herself. I know I should not allow it."

"You are the one who does not give any thought to putting yourself in danger," Mica said softly.

As Lena watched her cousin stand and leave the room, Obi-Wan thought he caught a first glimpse of tension and fear on her face. He looked at Qui-Gon to see if he too had noticed it, but Qui-Gon had retreated inside himself once more and was gazing into his tea cup.

"I'm sorry," Lena apologized, suddenly placing her hand to her brow. "I'm wasting your time, and I have not been entirely honest."

Obi-Wan sat up and Qui-Gon placed his cup on the table. They did not speak, but waited for Lena to continue.

"It is true that I need an escort to Coruscant. And it is true that I wish to testify against the Cobral. I must complete the task that Rutin started. The task he died for." Lena's voice caught and she stood, turning toward the shrouded windows before continuing. "In so many ways it is my fault. I did not mean to fall in love with him. I did not know he was a Cobral. But love isn't a choice, is it?"

Obi-Wan thought he saw Qui-Gon nod slightly.

"Before we married, Rutin promised he could stop the crime, but he could not stand to be cast out of his family. He was his parents' favorite and he loved them. He hoped that he could convince them to change their ways. He was not content to remove himself; he wanted to stop it all." Lena spoke more quickly as she went on, as if she could not stop the flow of words.

"But then his brother Solan found out that

Rutin was trying to change things. Furious, he went to their father. Rutin could not close the crime ring from the inside. So he decided to try to close it from the outside. It was the hardest decision he ever made. I wanted him to get out, but I begged him not to risk his life. He insisted. For me, he said. He did it for me." Lena paused again and turned back toward the Jedi. Her dark eyes were moist with tears.

Obi-Wan felt she was looking only at him, and her eyes bore straight into his heart. It was as if she were searching him, checking to see if he had the strength and courage to help her. If he could be trusted.

Obi-Wan knew instinctively that he trusted her. There was something about the way she carried herself, about the way she spoke. She was not lying to them. He could sense her fear, yes, but also her honesty. And he could feel her strength. Lena Cobral was not a coward.

"That is why I must carry out his plan," Lena said, straightening. "I can't let Rutin's death be for nothing. I will testify, I will stop the crime. But . . ."

Obi-Wan leaned in. So far the story was as he expected. But what?

"I don't have any solid evidence to bring before the Senate." Lena sighed. "Rutin worked very hard to protect me. Although I have heard many things, as all Fregans have, I have only my word against theirs."

Qui-Gon stood. Obi-Wan could tell by the look on his face that he was not happy about being fooled. They were sent to escort a witness in danger and now it seemed their witness had no testimony.

"Please," Lena said, taking Qui-Gon's large hand. "I beg you, stay until I have the proper evidence. I know it exists — lists and dates, accounts and records of the Cobrals' crimes. With your help —"

"We were sent only to protect you. If you cannot testify we must return to Coruscant alone," Qui-Gon said flatly.

Obi-Wan flushed, unable to believe what he was hearing. How could Qui-Gon deny this woman help?

CHAPTER 3

"Master!" Obi-Wan said, more sharply than he'd intended. "I —" He stopped, realizing that it would not be good to discuss their differing opinions in front of Lena. "I would like to speak with you," he finished.

Obi-Wan nodded to Lena and walked quickly toward the stairs and down one flight. Qui-Gon's footsteps followed. When he reached the landing, Obi-Wan whirled.

"Master, you can't mean to leave this woman here. She is obviously scared and in danger!" he burst out.

"She lied to us about having evidence, Obi-Wan. Who's to say she is not lying about the danger as well?" Qui-Gon said calmly.

"Her fear is real," Obi-Wan said. "Surely you can feel that. We cannot abandon her." His face felt warm. He had not spoken so strongly to his Master since before Tahl's death, but since then

Qui-Gon seemed to feel nothing outside of himself.

Qui-Gon gazed at his Padawan for some time. Obi-Wan did not look away. He would not allow Qui-Gon to walk away from this.

"We can stay for two days, that is all. If she does not have the evidence by that time we will return to Coruscant without her," Qui-Gon decided. "But I do not think this is a good idea. You are letting your emotions guide you."

"I will not regret it," Obi-Wan said tightly.

"That is my hope," his Master replied.

Anger and frustration welled up inside Obi-Wan. He started back up the stairs without another word. Hadn't Qui-Gon let his emotions guide him in the past? If only his Master would allow himself to feel some of those emotions now he would understand. They were making the right decision. Lena — and Frego — needed them.

Struggling to let go of his frustration, Obi-Wan paused before reentering the living quarters. Lena heard the Jedi on the stairs and turned. Her face was full of hope.

"We will stay two days," Obi-Wan told her with a smile.

"We will protect you while we are here, but that is all. We will not gather evidence against the Cobral," Qui-Gon added.

It was enough. Lena threw her arms around Obi-Wan's neck. "Thank you," she said in his ear. "Thank you. It is more than I can ask."

Obi-Wan felt his face and neck grow warm as he hugged Lena back awkwardly. Out of the corner of his eye he saw Qui-Gon and, behind him, Mica. Neither of them were smiling.

"Two days will be plenty, but there is no time to waste," Lena said. She dashed from the room and returned a moment later with a robe similar to Mica's. She quickly coiled her hair and pinned it on her head before covering it with a hood.

"I'm coming with you," Mica stated.

Lena shook her head. "There's no reason to put you in danger, too."

Obi-Wan thought he saw a flicker of annoyance in Mica's expression, but she was silent as the Jedi and Lena left the apartment.

Lena's manner was very brusque and her expression one of pure determination as she led the Jedi outside into the alley. Obi-Wan noticed her brows were drawn before she covered them with a pair of dark goggles that hid most of her face.

Lena moved through the streets even faster than her cousin. She led the Jedi from the dark, towering warehouses to a neighborhood filled with tall, sparkling buildings. Bubblelike turbolifts silently glided up and down their outside walls.

Lena came to an abrupt halt a dozen meters away from a particularly large and grand-looking building. Three imposing men stood on guard outside the bubble turbolift.

"We'll have to go in the back way," Lena said, finally turning toward the Jedi. She sighed sadly. "I haven't been back to my apartment since —"

"Your apartment?" Qui-Gon interrupted.

Obi-Wan guessed that his Master was not entirely surprised about their destination, but that he didn't think going inside was a good idea. Obi-Wan wasn't sure it was, either. But he wanted to help Lena.

"Are you certain that's wise?" Qui-Gon finished.

"We have no choice," Lena explained. "There's vital information inside. I need it to testify."

Qui-Gon did not reply as Lena turned and made her way down a narrow alley to a back entrance. Luckily this one was not guarded. Lena punched a code into a small panel and the door slid open. But there was no turbolift on this side of the building. They had to walk up thirty-seven flights of stairs.

By the time they reached the top floor, all of

them were out of breath. But Lena did not pause to rest. Instead she led them around a corner to what looked like a duracrete wall. It wasn't until he got up close that Obi-Wan realized it was actually a concealed door. Lena pressed a small button concealed inside a panel, and the door slid open.

Before Obi-Wan could even get a look inside, Lena gasped and put a hand to her mouth. They were standing in what had once been a beautiful parlor. But the apartment had been ransacked, and piles of debris littered the floor. Everything was ruined.

The rich fabrics that had covered the furniture were torn to shreds and strewn across the rooms. Tables and bureaus were smashed. Drawers were overturned and shelves cleared, their ripped and broken contents randomly spread across every surface.

The apartment had been lavishly decorated, but now it looked like the inside of a garbage scow. Whoever was responsible for the ransacking had done a thorough job. Even the carpets had been pulled up and hacked to pieces.

Beside him, Lena leaned heavily on Obi-Wan's arm. "I should have guessed that they would search," she said, forlorn. She leaned down and picked up the pieces of a small stone carving. She turned them over in her hand, and her eyes welled with tears. Obi-Wan wanted to comfort her, but wasn't sure what to say. He squeezed her arm gently.

"I suppose you should be glad you weren't at home," Qui-Gon replied dryly. He obviously hadn't noticed Lena's expression, and Obi-Wan felt a flash of annoyance. How could his Master be so insensitive?

Lena drew a deep breath and let go of Obi-Wan before picking her way carefully through the mess toward the back of the apartment. Qui-Gon stayed near the lift doors. Obi-Wan followed close behind Lena, in case she needed his support again. The apartment did not look like it had been searched so much as destroyed.

Her face full of sadness, Lena surveyed the damage. She paused once to pick up a trinket that was not entirely shattered, then placed it on a shelf still barely attached to the wall. Obi-Wan wondered how long it would stay there before sliding off.

"How strange!" Lena exclaimed as she walked into her bedroom, at the end of a long hall. Nothing in this room had been touched. The furnishings stood upright. The bed was made. Even the portrait on the wall was straight.

Obi-Wan stepped closer to the portrait. It was a picture of Lena and Rutin. They stood together in front of a waterfall, their eyes locked on each other. Something about the portrait disturbed Obi-Wan, but before he could place the feeling, the portrait and the wall it was on swung aside to reveal a small office.

"It's where Rutin worked in the evenings," Lena explained, walking through the secret door. "All of his family files are stored here. I just can't believe that whoever searched the house didn't —" Lena trailed off as she activated the computer screen.

Blue light and horror shone on Lena's face as a message flashed on the screen:

YOU CANNOT STOP US. YOU CAN ONLY DIE TRYING.

CHAPTER 4

Qui-Gon entered the back room just in time to see the message flash a final time. Then the computer went dead.

Lena sank into a chair. "They've erased the evidence," she said. "They've erased everything."

For a moment Lena's determination was replaced by desperation. Qui-Gon was surprised to feel a similar desperation coming from Obi-Wan. He gazed at him thoughtfully. This was unusual behavior for his Padawan.

Qui-Gon turned his attention to the matter at hand. "Was the computer connected to a network of some kind?" he asked.

"I don't think so," Lena said. Then she shook her head firmly. "No. Rutin would not have kept the information here if it was."

"And no one else had access to the information?" Qui-Gon questioned.

"Well, the information was no secret within

the family. They all know what's going on, but they are careful not to leave a trail. Solan makes sure of that." Lena stood up and walked back into her bedroom, talking more to herself than the Jedi. "Still, Rutin managed to construct a trail. Any of them could, but Solan . . ."

Qui-Gon could see that Lena was already recovering from the setback. She was formulating a new plan. Qui-Gon could not help but admire her resolve. And yet, if she loved her husband as she claimed, she was remarkably strong in the aftermath of his death. He thought perhaps she was deceiving them.

"They all know," Lena said again, louder. "And one of them might just help." Lena turned and began picking her way back toward the lift.

"Come on," she beckoned the Jedi. "I may need your protection even more now. We're going to the Cobral Estate."

"Really?" Qui-Gon asked. "Are you sure that's the best plan of action?"

"Only my mother-in-law lives there now. She's not part of the family business. Taking the risk will be worth it. It has to be."

In the basement of the building, Lena and the Jedi climbed into a large landspeeder. Within moments they were zipping outside the city, toward the home of Lena's mother-in-law, Zanita Cobral.

"We've always gotten along," Lena explained as they skimmed the surface of the planet. "Rutin was her favorite son. He was the youngest. Losing him was devastating for her, for all of us."

Qui-Gon had trouble focusing his attention on Lena from his seat in the rear. As he forced himself to stay present, in the back of his mind he wondered if coming on this mission had been a bad idea. It called for subtle judgments he wasn't certain he was equipped to make. He felt as if he was moving through a fog of unclear emotions.

"Zanita may be the only person on the planet who is not under Solan's thumb," Lena said to Obi-Wan. "She's the only one who can help. I just hope she wants to."

The Cobral Estate sat on a high ridge overlooking Rian. When the large home was within sight Lena activated a transparisteel roof, which quickly covered the travelers. Then she pushed another button and the transparisteel turned a dark shade of gray.

"When we reach the gate you'll have to duck down," Lena said. "The Cobrals don't like strangers."

Qui-Gon wondered how much the Cobrals would like seeing Lena. Even though she'd said that she and her mother-in-law were on good terms, her presence might stir things up rather than settle them.

At least they had someone to remind them of Rutin. But who did Qui-Gon have to remind him of Tahl? No one had known her as he had. Fresh memories came to him every day. There was no one to share them with.

Crouched in the back and covered by his own robe, Qui-Gon felt Lena tense. He could tell it was not just apprehension about the meeting with Zanita. Something else was happening.

"That's Solan's speeder," she whispered to the Jedi. "And his brother Bard's. The whole family is here."

Qui-Gon raised his head enough to see a number of luxury vehicles parked in the bay outside the mansion. There was no doubt that the Cobrals possessed extraordinary wealth.

"Maybe we should come back later," Obi-Wan suggested gently from the front seat.

"No. I don't have time," Lena said with her familiar resolve. "We'll sneak in, and I'll find a way to get Zanita alone. Or maybe I'll find what I need on my own and we won't need her help after all. We might be able to get additional information. Having several of the Cobrals present could turn out to be a good thing. "

Or a deadly one, Qui-Gon thought.

Lena parked her speeder at the far end of the row, next to a metal statue.

"We can get in through the galley," she said, motioning with her head toward a small entrance.

Qui-Gon watched as Lena and Obi-Wan moved silently into position by the galley door. Moments later a cooking servant emerged. He did not notice as Lena slipped her foot into the door, preventing it from closing. When the servant rounded the edge of the building, Qui-Gon slipped into the galley after Lena and Obi-Wan.

The entrance had been too easy.

The cooking quarters were vast, with rows of gleaming countertops and food storage units. Servants bustled about, busily preparing a large meal.

Lena waited until most of the servants had their backs to the door, then pulled up her hood and walked through the quarters. She carried herself with such authority that nobody bothered to ask who she was or where she was going.

Soon after entering a spectacularly long hallway covered in lush, thick carpet, she ducked into a small room and pulled Obi-Wan and Qui-Gon in after her. The room held several holo-screens.

"This used to be a guard station," Lena explained. "But when her husband died Zanita didn't think she needed as much protection, so it's no longer used."

Qui-Gon felt slightly relieved. At least there was an explanation for the easy entrance.

Lena adjusted one of the holoscreens until it showed a large dining room filled with people.

"It's Bard's birthday," Lena said with relief. A large Fregan birth celebration banner lay across the dining table. "I should have remembered."

The crowd milled about the room, smiling and carrying glasses filled with red liquid. At first glance it looked like any other party. Qui-Gon looked harder.

"There's Zanita," Lena said, pointing to a tall older woman dressed in a black gown covered in tiny smokats. A large scarf was wrapped attractively around her head like a turban. In spite of her age she was easily the most striking person in the room. Qui-Gon was surprised by her commanding presence and the way she set people around her at ease — laughing, smiling, and making sure they were taken care of. Then something else caught his eye.

"Is that Solan?" he asked quietly, pointing at a scowling man in the corner.

"Yes, how did you know?" Lena asked.

Qui-Gon raised his eyebrows but said nothing. His eyes stayed trained on Solan. Like Zanita, the frowning man was surrounded by a large group of people. But none of the people near Solan seemed to be enjoying his company. They simply stood nervously by.

Suddenly Solan stood. A woman next to him rushed to take his empty cup and napkin. Someone else asked if they could get anything for him, but he brushed them off with a wave of his hand. Solan approached the guest of honor, a man shorter than him but who otherwise bore a striking resemblance to him. It was the middle brother, Bard.

Casually tossing an arm over Bard's shoulder, Solan interrupted the conversation and steered him toward the outer edges of the party. He spoke in hushed tones.

"They're all afraid of him," Obi-Wan remarked.

Qui-Gon was glad to see the stiffening shoulders of the younger brother had not escaped the attention of his apprentice. "Exactly," said Qui-Gon. "Even his family is fearful."

Lena held up a hand to silence the Jedi. "Zanita's leaving the party," she whispered. "This is my chance."

Without another word Lena slipped out the door, leaving the Jedi to watch her on the holoscreen. She made her way down the long hallway toward the library. It was a large room, with towering shelves of important-looking books and polished furniture. Zanita was inside, apparently taking a moment to relax.

Qui-Gon felt a strange unease. In spite of Zanita's pleasing manner he did not think the meeting would go well.

Obi-Wan leaned close to the screen. Lena entered the library unseen by the other guests.

The look on Zanita's face when she saw her daughter-in-law was one of sheer pleasure. The older woman stood and embraced Lena, holding her close for a long time.

Obi-Wan fiddled with the projection controls beneath the screen, tuning out the party guests until all they heard were the voices of Lena and Zanita in the library.

"But, my dear, why would you hide from your family?" Zanita asked, her voice filled with concern.

"I was afraid," Lena explained. "And without Rutin, I didn't know what you would think of me."

"You will always be a Cobral," Zanita said solemnly, looking thoughtfully at her daughter-in-law. "But why were you afraid?"

Lena hesitated, then lowered her voice. "I

am afraid because I think Solan had Rutin killed."

Zanita staggered back before sinking onto a large, comfortable-looking sofa. Her skin paled and she reached a shaking hand toward Lena.

"It was my greatest fear," Zanita whispered as tears sprang to her eyes. "I did not want it to be true. And yet, when I look into my heart, I know you are not lying."

She pulled a piece of embroidered cloth from her pocket and wiped her eyes before going on. "I tried to stop Solan, to make him see reason, but it was too late," she sobbed again. "And now Rutin is gone."

Kneeling beside her, Lena comforted Zanita as best she could. She also told Zanita all she knew of Rutin's plan to end the crime ring. "I know it will not be easy for you to hear, but now I am planning to testify against the family. Rutin's dearest wish has become mine as well. I want to stop the violence," Lena explained, looking into her mother-in-law's eyes. "And I need your help."

In the guard room, Qui-Gon detected a slight quaver in Lena's voice. He could not fault her, of course. She was asking Zanita to join her in betraying her own family — her own children.

Zanita kept her eyes on her lap, but let go of Lena's hand. Her commanding presence

seemed somehow diminished as she sat un-
moving on the sofa. At last she looked up at the
portrait hanging on the library wall. It was a picture of three men, the Cobral brothers. Rutin
stood proudly in the center.

"Yes," she breathed. "It must stop."

CHAPTER 5

Zanita sat quietly for another long moment. When she looked up, there were tears in her eyes. "There is a set of documents," she said slowly. "I think I can get them for you. But you must promise me that you will not link my name to the testimony in any way."

"Of course not, Zanita," Lena assured her. She squeezed her mother-in-law's shoulder. "I know the violence and corruption are not your doing."

Zanita seemed to become empowered while her mind worked. It reminded Qui-Gon of Lena. "It will take me some time to get the documents. Perhaps by tomorrow night," she said. "I must be very, very careful. If Solan were to suspect —"

Suddenly a loud voice boomed just outside the library door. Qui-Gon's face registered concern. It was a man's voice, and it sounded angry.

Lena let go of her mother-in-law's arm and put a finger to her lips. Without wasting a second she got to her feet and ducked behind a heavy curtain covering the library's transparisteel portal.

A moment later the door slid open and Solan thundered into the room. "Mother," he said sternly, looking at her as if she were a child who needed scolding. "What are you doing in here?"

Zanita looked evenly at her son. She was not a child, and it appeared that she did not appreciate being treated like one. "I was just having a moment to myself," she replied simply. Her face showed no sign of fear.

Solan tapped his foot on the floor impatiently. "You are the hostess of your son's birthday celebration," he stated. "It is not appropriate for you to slip away to have a moment to yourself. If necessary you can do that when the party is over."

"Stop bullying me, Solan. This is my house, and I'll do as I like." She looked her son in the face.

Solan blinked and stepped backward. "Juno needs you in the kitchen," he said more quietly. "He is not clear about which service platters you would like to use for dinner."

"Fine. I will go and discuss it with him," Zanita replied.

"Good. Then come back to the party."

Zanita did not acknowledge the fact that her son had just given her an order. Instead she followed him easily out of the library. She did not turn around as the door quietly closed behind her.

After waiting a few moments, Lena left the room as well. Minutes later she met up with the Jedi in the guard station.

"I assume you heard all of that," she said. "He infuriates me, talking to his own mother like that. Sometimes I wish she'd really put him in his place." Her voice quieted. "But I suppose that might get her killed."

Lena paused while her quick mind moved on to the next thought. Her eyes were suddenly lit with excitement. Qui-Gon wasn't sure if it was the thrill of escape or the result of the meeting with her mother-in-law.

"Isn't it great?" she asked, perhaps a little too brightly. "Zanita is going to help us. I knew she would. Leave it to a woman to understand that the violent ways of the crime world can only lead to destruction and hate."

Qui-Gon could not help but think of Jenna Zan Arbor, a mad female scientist who had conducted horrible experiments on live human subjects — including him. He knew many women who lived lives of crime and violence. But he didn't say anything.

"Anyway, I'm very relieved. The meeting couldn't have gone better."

"It does look as though your mother-in-law is willing to help you get testimony," Qui-Gon agreed. "Let's just hope she keeps her word."

Lena nodded as she turned back to the security screens. "We still have to get out of here without being discovered," she said. She looked at each screen in turn, noting the whereabouts of everyone in the house. Qui-Gon knew she was trying to figure out the best time to leave.

"Follow me," Lena said after a moment. She slid open the guard station door and peered into the hallway. She motioned to the Jedi, and they all stepped out of the room. Zanita was still in the cooking quarters with Juno, so they left through another, rarely used entrance at the side of the mansion.

As they made their way outside, Qui-Gon considered the Cobral family. On the surface they appeared like any other family — close and loving, but not without tension. Beneath the surface, however, lay dark ties. There was fear there, and possibly hatred as well.

Of course, this did not entirely surprise Qui-

Gon. A family that ruled a planet with corruption and violence was bound to have a sinister web woven within it.

Distracted by his own thoughts, Qui-Gon did not sense any nearby danger. It was Obi-Wan who cried out first.

"Look out!" he shouted, pushing Qui-Gon and Lena away from their landspeeder.

As the three of them tumbled to the ground, a huge metal statue thundered down where they had been standing. It crashed into the front end of their landspeeder, missing them by mere centimeters.

Their vehicle was destroyed. And if not for a few seconds of warning, they might have been killed, too.

CHAPTER 6

The Jedi and Lena were still on the ground when Zanita and Juno came rushing out the cooking quarters door. Qui-Gon felt Lena tense at the sight of the servant, and for a brief moment Juno glared at her. But his face shifted quickly into a look of concern.

"Are you all right?" he asked, holding out a hand to help her up.

Lena got to her feet on her own and brushed herself off. "Fine," she replied briskly. She casually scanned the area to see if anyone else was coming. It was a good thing they had parked their vehicle on the opposite side of the mansion from the entertaining quarters.

Qui-Gon was impressed with Lena's composure. And he didn't need to glance at his Padawan to know that Obi-Wan was as well.

Zanita's turban was askew, and the older woman seemed slightly out of breath. But she did not show any surprise at the fact that Lena had come to her home with two companions she had never met.

"We really must strengthen the base of that statue," Juno said, eyeing the giant metal sculpture on the ground. "It's quite unsafe."

"Quite," Qui-Gon agreed dryly.

"Zanita, do you remember Obi-Wan Kenobi and Qui-Gon Jinn?" Lena asked, raising her eyebrows slightly at her mother-in-law. "They are friends of mine."

Qui-Gon knew instinctively that Lena was trying to lead her late husband's mother away from saying out loud, or even somehow suggesting, that she had never met them before. He guessed that this was because of Juno's presence.

"Of course," Zanita replied easily. "How nice to see you again."

Qui-Gon smiled with a graciousness he didn't feel. "And you as well," he said, taking her hand for a moment in the Fregan custom.

Juno appeared annoyed that he hadn't been introduced to the Jedi. Clearing his throat loudly, he stepped toward the group. "You must come inside and rest," he declared. "We have a medical droid who can examine you for injuries."

Qui-Gon tried not to grimace as he realized

that a family like the Cobrals probably *needed* its own medical droid. But there was something odd about Juno's offer. Qui-Gon was quite sure that in spite of the look of concern he wore, the servant was not truly worried about their welfare. Perhaps he had other motives for wanting to get the group back inside the house.

"I'm sure that won't be necessary, Juno," Zanita said pointedly. "Lena and her friends were just leaving." She looked around furtively. After the exchange with her son in the library, Qui-Gon guessed that the mention of going inside — or the possibility of someone coming out — made her nervous.

"You can borrow a landspeeder, Lena," she added. "It's the least I can do."

Lena smiled at her mother-in-law. "That would be most appreciated," she said. "Thank you, Zanita."

Juno scowled at Lena, then started off toward the vehicle storage building.

"Lena knows where the landspeeders are housed, Juno," Zanita said. "And she can take either of mine. You don't need to direct her."

Juno's frown deepened, but he didn't say anything.

"We'd best be getting back inside," Zanita said brightly when Juno didn't move. "We have guests to attend to."

With a last look at the three visitors, Juno turned and followed his employer back into the cooking quarters.

"Another close one," Lena whispered, shivering slightly. "Rutin never liked Juno, and he gives me the creeps." She eyed the door Juno and Zanita had just disappeared through, then turned and started toward the vehicle hangar. "Let's get out of here before something else happens."

Minutes later Lena and the Jedi were on their way back into the city.

"It was nice of Zanita to offer up her landspeeder," Obi-Wan noted from the front seat.

"Very nice," Lena agreed. But she did not say anything else. She suddenly seemed to focus very hard on piloting the speeder.

Once again in the backseat, Qui-Gon considered the events of the last few hours. Though he didn't particularly want to admit it, he felt at a loss. He was not able to decipher whether Zanita or Lena were being honest — either with each other or himself and Obi-Wan.

Qui-Gon sighed. For the millionth time he wished that Tahl were still alive. Aside from the aching absence that still burned inside him, he knew that her sharp perception and intuition would uncover the truth. She would not be distracted by the composed, polished surfaces of these women. She would cut through all of that and get to their real intentions, their motives.

Qui-Gon bowed his head and tried to let the grief of missing Tahl move through him. Isn't that what Yoda had taught him — what he had repeatedly told his Padawan?

Allow yourself to feel the emotions, then let them go. Qui-Gon focused on the words. He felt the grief well up inside him until he was sure it would break him, shatter him to pieces. Then, with every nerve of his body, he tried to let the pain go.

It wouldn't.

His head aching, Qui-Gon opened his eyes. It was always the same. He felt the incredible fullness of the pain, and then endless hollowness. The grief never actually left. It emptied him, but it would not leave him alone.

CHAPTER 7

Obi-Wan was silent as the landspeeder traveled through the city. He could sense his Master's melancholy mood, and Lena was attentive only to driving. She navigated skillfully through the city, and Obi-Wan was yet again impressed by her composure. Less than half an hour ago they had nearly been killed. Yet she seemed to have wiped the memory away as easily as one wipes a crumb from a table.

Obi-Wan had assumed that they were going back to Lena's warehouse hideout. Instead she turned off toward her ransacked apartment after making sure they were not being followed. Obi-Wan considered inquiring about this, but thought better of it. He guessed that Lena was being silent for a reason.

Lena parked the landspeeder several hundred meters away from her building. They approached carefully, and found only one guard outside the turbolift. He was dozing off. Moving quickly past him, they entered the turbolift and were whisked to the top floor. Once inside her flat, Lena moved through room after room at a rapid pace, the Jedi at her heels.

Qui-Gon did not say anything, but followed with assurance. Obi-Wan felt a moment of frustration as he realized that his Master was not experiencing the same confusion he was. Even in his depressed state he seemed to know exactly what was going on.

It took a bit of effort for Obi-Wan to keep up with the two people in front of him. Lena led them out the secret exit they had used before, then down flight after flight of stairs. She did not slow her pace when they reached the alley. She simply hurried down several blocks, turning this way and that. Finally she hailed an air taxi and they all climbed inside.

Relieved not to be chasing after Lena and his Master, Obi-Wan sat back against the seat. "Were we being followed?" he asked. It was the logical reason for Lena's actions.

"Not that I know of," Lena said in a strange tone. She sounded almost giddy, as if the idea were amusing. "Zanita is really a wonderful woman. I'm lucky to know her."

Obi-Wan thought it was strange that Lena was speaking about her mother-in-law as if they were acquaintances and not family. But once again he kept quiet. What did he know about families, anyway?

Lena told the taxi driver to let them off several blocks from the warehouse. Once they were walking again, she relaxed a little. A moment later she reached out and touched Obi-Wan's arm.

"Sorry about that," she said, looking into his eyes. Obi-Wan tried to ignore the way he felt when she gazed at him.

"I couldn't talk in the taxi because of the sky drivers' collective," she explained. "They are Cobral supporters. And as for Zanita's vehicle, well, let's just say that it has plenty of added surveillance equipment that even Zanita might not know about."

Obi-Wan nodded, and Lena turned and kept walking. She spoke quietly, but loud enough for both Obi-Wan and Qui-Gon to hear.

"That statue falling was no accident. I'm sure the base is completely secure, no matter what Juno says. There are several traps on the property — the Cobrals call it security. They say they have to protect what's theirs."

"Who do you think triggered it?" Qui-Gon asked, speaking for the first time since they'd left the Cobral property.

"I don't know," Lena replied. "The Cobrals

have many allies — paid and unpaid. Although Juno is Zanita's servant, he works for Solan first. I'm sure he would be handsomely rewarded if he succeeded in killing me."

The group's mood was contemplative as they navigated the streets and arrived back at the warehouse.

Inside, Mica was pacing the living space. A medium-size package lay on a low table.

"This arrived while you were out," Mica said. She picked up the package and thrust it into her cousin's hands. She seemed slightly agitated.

Lena took the package and turned it over. It was covered in a thin gray wrapping material. There was nothing written on the material other than her name in block letters: LENA COBRAL.

CHAPTER 8

"Rutin," Lena said, gazing down at the package. She ran her fingers over her name. "This is Rutin's handwriting," she explained, looking up at the Jedi. "I'd recognize it anywhere."

Qui-Gon looked down at the package, feeling quite certain that it was some sort of trap. Rutin was dead, was he not?

"I'd like to have a look at that," he said, stepping forward. "I want to make sure it is not dangerous before you open it."

Lena frowned. "Rutin would never put me in danger," she said adamantly.

Qui-Gon raised an eyebrow. From what he could gather, Rutin had put her in significant danger. But he saw no point in reminding Lena of that now.

"It could be a trap," Qui-Gon said plainly.

Lena scowled slightly at Qui-Gon. Perhaps, Qui-Gon mused, she felt he was stealing her last gift from Rutin. But she gave Qui-Gon the package.

Closing his eyes, Qui-Gon held the package for several moments. When he opened them again, he returned the package to Lena.

"I do not sense anything immediately grave," he said. But he was not convinced that the package was from Rutin, or that it would help them gain evidence against the Cobral. He was not convinced of anything.

Lena set the box on the table and opened it with a small pocket blade before removing the wrapping. Then she began to empty its contents and set them on the table: a pair of black boots, a small vial of dirt . . . Lena's face fell as she looked over the contents of the box. "This doesn't make sense," she murmured.

"I think I'll go make us all something to eat," Mica said, excusing herself.

"Good idea, Mica," Lena said. "I'm starved."

Qui-Gon sat down next to Lena as soon as Mica left the room. He was unclear about the motives of both women, but felt he might be able to get some answers if he addressed them individually.

"Have you had any visitors to the warehouse?" he asked, not wasting any time.

Lena turned her attention away from the package and shook her head. "No, why?"

Instead of answering, Qui-Gon asked another question. "Have you received mysterious packages before today?"

Lena shook her head again. "No, of course not. I would have told you about them."

"I'm glad to hear that," Qui-Gon said, not entirely sure that he believed her.

The next question was perhaps the most important. "Is Mica the only one who knows about this place?" he asked quietly.

Lena looked up quickly. She was frowning.

"I think I'll go see if Mica needs any help with the food," Obi-Wan said abruptly.

Qui-Gon gave a brief nod to his Padawan, indicating that he thought it was a good idea. But he did not take his eyes off Lena's face.

Still frowning, Lena got to her feet. "Yes, Mica is the only other person besides you and Obi-Wan who knows about this apartment," she said flatly. She turned to face Qui-Gon again, her hands on her hips. "But do not question my cousin's loyalty. Mica and I grew up together. We are like sisters. And she is not in league with the Cobrals."

Lena crossed the room, then let out a sigh and came back to sit next to Qui-Gon. "I don't even like to discuss the Cobrals in front of Mica," she said slowly. "As a very young girl she witnessed the murder of her mother, and the memory is still excruciatingly painful."

"The Cobrals were responsible for her mother's death?" Qui-Gon asked, slightly surprised.

Lena nodded sadly. "They killed her in cold blood. Mica was only seven and she saw the whole thing. It was a huge loss, and perhaps an even bigger trauma. She has never gotten over it."

Qui-Gon was silent as this information sank in.

"Everything on Frego is so complicated," Lena said with a heavy sigh. "But I will try to explain. As I've said before, the Cobrals have many allies on Frego. For centuries Frego's government treated the citizens poorly — taxes were high and public services virtually nonexistent. Fregans worked hard only to have their money taken from them.

"The Cobral family changed all of that. While it is true that they made their fortune selling drugs and weapons and had a rough reputation, they used their power to force the government to provide the basic services people needed. They even lowered taxes and raised wages."

"Which made life for the people better," Qui-Gon said. He had visited planets with similar stories. A corrupt power ousted an unjust government, making positive changes. But the means through which those positive changes were made had its own kind of evil.

"Today the government acknowledges that the ways of the past were wrong, that they treated the people unfairly," Lena continued. "And many politicians resent having to operate under the Cobral thumb. They want to do right by their people. Or at least some of them do. Others appear to be noble, but are corrupt to the core."

"I see that the Cobral makes things quite complicated," Qui-Gon commented. "For everyone, it seems."

"There is no honesty, no safety," Lena stated. "We live by whims and not laws. That is why the violence has to stop. I know there is a better way, and I want Frego to have a chance for a new beginning — the beginning that Rutin and I did not have."

Tears welled in Lena's eyes, and for the first time Qui-Gon softened toward her. He understood just how she felt. He and Tahl had never had a new beginning, either.

Lena wiped her cheek. "There are some politicians who would also like to forge a new path for the future. And some people would like to support a new government. But many others feel a strong debt to the Cobrals for making life better."

Lena gazed solemnly at the package and the boots on the table. "It seems that no one can break free."

"But you trust your cousin completely?" Qui-Gon asked, getting back to his original line of questioning.

Lena looked Qui-Gon in the eye. "Without hesitation. As I told you, she is like my sister. Mica longs to avenge her mother and shed the corruption. Perhaps more than anyone."

Qui-Gon did not point out that Rutin and Solan were brothers. Instead he took a breath and let it out slowly.

"I'm afraid that Mica may have revealed your whereabouts," he stated. "Or else another party has discovered them on their own."

CHAPTER 9

Obi-Wan entered the food galley and was only half surprised to see that the room was empty. Turning back down the hall, he spotted an old turbolift in one of the makeshift bedrooms. A second later he felt the building shudder. Mica was running away.

Obi-Wan leaped into the turbolift shaft, landing gracefully on top of the lift just as it came to a halt. Activating his lightsaber, he sliced a hole in the metal and jumped down a second time. But the lift was already empty. He heard the echo of Mica's receding footsteps as she raced toward the door.

Obi-Wan knew he should continue to follow her . . . doing so could provide information vital to the mission, and to Lena. What if Mica was out to hurt her cousin — what if her actions put Lena in even greater danger?

He couldn't risk that. He had to talk to Mica. Now.

It did not take Obi-Wan long to catch up to the girl. Grabbing her arm, he was struck by the anger he felt well up inside him. He was furious, he realized, because Mica was jeopardizing Lena's safety.

Obi-Wan calmed himself, intending to let the anger leave him before speaking. But as soon as he saw Mica's face the anger disappeared. The girl was clearly distraught.

"Where are you going?" Obi-Wan asked, trying not to sound too stern.

Mica looked alarmed. "I . . . I was . . ." She blinked, her eyes glistening with tears. "I need to go somewhere," she finished in a whisper.

"Not before you tell me what's going on," Obi-Wan said. He spotted several large crates in a corner and led her over to them. Sitting her down on one, he found another for himself.

"It's time for you to tell the truth. If you truly care about Lena, you'll do so," he said.

Mica looked down at her feet. She didn't say anything for several minutes. Then she started to talk. "The Cobral is terrible," she began. "They do hideous, evil things. But I do not think that Lena — or anyone else — is capable of bringing them down. Rutin tried, and he is dead. Killed by his own family. My mother was killed by the Cobral as well."

A sob escaped Mica's throat and she wiped her eyes. "Of course I want to avenge her death. And I know that she is not the only one. Mine is not the only loss. I long to see those killers pay for their crimes. But if I go after them I would probably be killed, too. And so would Lena. They think nothing of taking life. It means nothing to them. Not even in their own family."

Obi-Wan nodded. "I cannot tell you that you are wrong," he said. "But the Cobral has Frego caught in an evil trap of violence and crime. Lena has a chance to destroy that trap — and those who made it — for good. She is willing to take that chance."

Mica nodded. "I know. Lena is a hero. She thinks nothing of her own life, only of Frego and its people. And I am nothing but a coward, guilty of thwarting her plan."

Obi-Wan nodded again, surprised that he was not filled with anger for a second time. He knew that Mica had been deceiving Lena but he was somehow relieved that Mica felt guilty about her actions. "How?" he asked simply.

"I wanted to stop the trial," Mica explained. "It was too dangerous. So I convinced Lena to wait until you arrived before proceeding with her plan. Then I broke into her apartment and erased the files. I figured that if the evidence was gone, Lena would have to give up. And if she gave up, the Cobral would leave her alone. She would be safe. Of course, I did not expect to find the hired thugs at her apartment."

"Thugs?" Obi-Wan repeated.

Mica nodded. "They were heavily armed and ransacking the place. At the time I thought they were just street people, thieves after the jewelry and precious metals. Lena and Rutin had a lot of beautiful possessions."

She paused for a moment before going on. "But then I realized that they must have been searching for something."

"Did you see what they looked like?" Obi-Wan asked.

"No," Mica said. "They fled as soon as they heard me coming. They left the bedroom alone. I only caught a glimpse of their backs as they climbed over the balcony. I did not try to get a better look because I didn't want them to see me. I only know that there were two of them — both men. One was quite tall and lanky. The other short and bald."

"Not much to go on," Obi-Wan mused.

"I'm sure they were hired by the Cobral," Mica said.

Obi-Wan felt better about Mica now that she had confided in him. But there was still one question that was bothering him. "I understand why you wanted to erase the computer files, but why did you leave that threatening message on the screen?"

Mica looked up, surprised. "What message?" she asked. "I didn't send any message." She paused for a moment. Then, as if reading Obi-Wan's mind, she said, "And I didn't tell anyone where Lena was hiding, either."

CHAPTER 10

Lena looked at Qui-Gon in disbelief. Qui-Gon could tell she did not think Mica would reveal her whereabouts, but the package on the table meant it was likely that someone had. The strange contents were not dangerous, but the knowledge of Lena's whereabouts was — especially in the wrong hands.

"I must speak to Obi-Wan." Qui-Gon excused himself.

Walking slowly toward the kitchen, Qui-Gon felt exhausted. This routine mission was turning out to be more difficult than he'd imagined. He felt a strong sense of deception, but something about it continued to elude him. He could not tell who was being deceived, or by whom. And he did not understand why Lena so fiercely protected her cousin. She had obviously learned — the hard way — that family lines do not protect you from being double-crossed. Or killed.

The food galley was empty. Following his instincts, Qui-Gon started down the stairs. Halfway to the ground level, Qui-Gon met Obi-Wan and a sullen Mica coming up the stairwell.

"The evidence is gone," Obi-Wan blurted. "Mica erased it."

"Erased or stole?" Qui-Gon asked, looking directly at Mica.

"Erased!" Mica spat back defiantly. "I do not profit by the misfortune of others, especially Lena." Her voice softened when she spoke of her cousin. "I only wanted to protect her. To make all of this go away." Mica hung her head and shuffled her feet before the Jedi led her back up the stairs. She obviously knew it was time to tell Lena what she had done.

Although she was clearly ashamed of her actions, Qui-Gon felt that her conscience was clear. She was not deceiving them. He felt relief in knowing that *somebody* wasn't.

"Obi-Wan." Qui-Gon stopped his Padawan on the landing, allowing Mica to go farther ahead. "We must proceed with caution. All is not as it seems with our witness. On this planet, lies come easier than the truth, and at a lower cost."

As Obi-Wan raised his eyes to meet his

Master's, Qui-Gon saw tiny flames of anger burn inside them, then flicker out.

"Lena is a noble woman," Obi-Wan said evenly. "She is struggling to do what is right. Your doubts will not help her."

Qui-Gon could not help but smile faintly. Obi-Wan thought Qui-Gon was insulting Lena, and he was upset — ready to defend her. It confirmed what Qui-Gon had suspected, that Obi-Wan was infatuated with Lena. He should have pointed it out sooner, to try and warn the boy. Most likely he would end up getting badly hurt.

"You are infatuated, Obi-Wan," Qui-Gon said. "Be careful not to let yourself be guided by your attraction."

"I am —" Obi-Wan shook his head and struggled to keep his voice under control. "It is not infatuation. Lena's motives are good."

"The motives she has told us are good, but there may be others. Think of what she is giving up. She will probably never live again in the manner to which she was accustomed. She lost her footing with the Cobral when Rutin was killed and is in danger of being an outcast. Not just from the family, but from all of Frego. Don't you think it is possible that she is trying to get evidence in order to have something to bargain with?"

Obi-Wan made no gesture to show that he

understood. "There is another day," he said softly. "Then we shall see." He turned to walk up the stairs.

Qui-Gon entered Lena's quarters behind his apprentice. Mica stood over the table staring at an empty box. The contents of the package were gone.

"I told her I erased the evidence," Mica said tearfully. "But I don't think she even heard me."

"Where is Lena now?" Qui-Gon asked. Obi-Wan was already headed for the stairs.

"I don't know," Mica sobbed, sinking into a low couch. "She didn't say anything to me. She just took what was in the box and left."

CHAPTER 11

"Obi-Wan, wait," his Master commanded. Obi-Wan did not want to listen. Not now. Not while Lena was alone and in danger. But he slid to a stop at the top of the stairs.

"We'll have a better chance of finding her if we have some idea where she might have gone," Qui-Gon said. He sat down next to Mica. "Where do *you* think she went?" he asked evenly.

Obi-Wan remained at the top of the stairs. He knew his impatience had little to do with finding Lena. He was impatient with his Master, and a bit confused. He used to know Qui-Gon so well that at times it felt like they shared one mind. They both knew how the other would react to a situation, what his thoughts and actions would be. But this was no longer the case.

Just when Obi-Wan believed that Qui-Gon was beyond caring about the mission, he had taken charge. If Qui-Gon hadn't stopped Obi-Wan, he would be with Lena now, and sure of her safety. Leaning against the stair railing, Obi-Wan let out an exasperated sigh. There was no point in questioning Mica.

"Let's go, then," Qui-Gon said. He stood and strode toward the stairs in fluid movement. Mica, eyes still red from crying, hurried in front of him.

Obi-Wan followed. He had been too lost in his own thoughts to hear where they were headed. Breathing deeply, he let go of his frustration and focused his energy on the matter at hand. Qui-Gon had no right to doubt Lena. He had been too distracted until now to even notice who she was, her real nature. But if Qui-Gon was — at least for the moment — concentrating on the mission, Obi-Wan could too.

Mica was not as concerned with being seen this time as she led the Jedi through the streets of Rian. They left the warehouses and alleys and hurried into the center of the city. Over Qui-Gon's head Obi-Wan saw a gleaming transparent structure, like an enormous serpent that snaked its way overhead, between the towering buildings.

Inside the structure Obi-Wan saw green leaves and moving forms. Water beaded on the inside of the rounded transparisteel walls, making it look like a vast, multistoried greenhouse. Although Obi-Wan could not see where it began or where it ended, the structure appeared to wind through the city for several kilometers.

"There," an out-of-breath Mica said, pointing toward a door to the structure. "I think she might be in the Tubal Park."

"I was hoping for something a bit smaller," Qui-Gon said. Obi-Wan could not tell if he was mildly amused or truly frustrated.

Obi-Wan caught up to Mica as they approached the entrance. "Why would she come here?" he asked.

"This park means a lot to Lena. She used to come here with Rutin, and she always comes here to think," Mica answered. "Or at least she used to."

The giant oval doors opened and the three stepped inside. As the doors closed behind them Obi-Wan felt as if he'd stepped off a ship onto another planet. Inside the air was moist. The noise of the city was gone, replaced by the echoing sound of running water and children's voices.

Looking up, Obi-Wan could only barely make out the seams in the roof beyond the tops of the towering trees. Paths crisscrossed one another, leading toward brightly blooming plants or meandering beside creeks and trickling waterfalls. People strolled over the bridges and ducked through the tunnels that wove under and around the dense flora. There were small animals winging overhead, and even smaller amphibians flopping in the pools.

Obi-Wan could see why Lena would come here. It reminded him of the Room of a Thousand Fountains at the Jedi Temple. That, too, was a sanctuary and a great place to go to think.

"Do you know her favorite spot?" Qui-Gon asked.

Mica shook her head sadly. "I never came here with her. She only came alone, or with Rutin. She could be anywhere."

"Then I suggest we split up," Qui-Gon said to Obi-Wan. "Mica can come with me."

Obi-Wan nodded and headed off to his left. It would be a relief to be away from Qui-Gon for a while. He could use some time alone to think.

As soon as he had walked away from his Master, Obi-Wan's mind filled with thoughts of Lena. All around him people were gathered in small groups. They ate, played, and leaned back on the grass to stare up at the leaves. Yet Obi-Wan was only aware of them enough to know that they were not Lena.

Could it really be infatuation? Obi-Wan wondered. After taking several deep breaths and letting go of his anger and frustration, Obi-Wan could not deny it. As usual, Qui-Gon was right. He was falling for Lena. But it was not just her beauty. No, it was more than that.

It was her strength — the strength she drew from her vulnerability — that had enamored him. Lena was a grieving young widow. The husband she had loved was only recently lost. But instead of hiding in the hole that he'd left, she pulled new purpose from it. She was not drowning in it, refusing to speak of the loss. Not like Qui-Gon.

Obi-Wan's thoughts drifted back to his Master. He shook his head as he climbed a steep bridge arching over a waterfall. Perhaps the bond between them was not as damaged as Obi-Wan imagined. No matter how he tried, Obi-Wan could not deny that Qui-Gon correctly recognized Obi-Wan's feelings for Lena, and before he did.

How can he be so clear about the emotions of others when he cannot seem to untangle his own? Obi-Wan wondered.

"With time," Master Yoda would say. "With time all are healed."

Obi-Wan felt new energy flood through him as he relaxed and let go of everything that had been bothering him. He had been in danger of letting his emotions blind him. Now he felt more sure.

Still, Obi-Wan did not believe his Master had been right about *everything*. Walking more quickly and scanning the park for Lena, Obi-Wan realized his resolve to help her was stronger than ever. Whether or not his judgment had been clouded by affection, he knew that Lena was on the side of rightness.

For the first time in hours, Obi-Wan felt clear. And he was more certain than ever that Lena was doing the right thing. She was fighting for peace and justice, and not just for herself. For her entire planet. As a Jedi it was his duty to help.

As these thoughts formed in his mind, a new one floated over them like a dark cloud:

They were running out of time.

CHAPTER 12

Qui-Gon pulled his comlink from his utility belt. He was about to activate it and summon Obi-Wan when his Padawan appeared, walking toward him on one of the paths.

"There he is," said Mica a moment later. She craned her neck to see what Qui-Gon already knew. Lena wasn't with him, either. The three of them had scoured most of the enormous park, but Lena was nowhere to be found.

Mica and the Jedi left the park and walked back to the deserted warehouse in silence. Qui-Gon tried to stretch out with his feelings, to get a sense of whether or not Lena was in danger, or even alive. But he felt nothing.

The dim evening light made the hideout look less welcoming than it had early that morning. Qui-Gon strode into the room ahead of the others, and immediately saw a figure sitting on the couch in the darkness.

In a flash, he activated his lightsaber. Its green blade cast an eerie light over the room, illuminating the sparks in Lena's eyes. Qui-Gon quickly switched off the blade just as Obi-Wan and Mica came into the room.

"Lena," Mica cried when she saw her cousin. She hurried forward and sank to her knees in front of the couch. "Lena, we were so worried. Where were you?"

"I'm sorry I ran off," Lena said, looking from one person to the next. "I didn't want to worry you, but I had to be sure that the package was from Rutin. I had to know. . . ." Lena trailed off.

Mica rose to turn on the light. Back on the table, next to the wrappings, were the contents of the package: the pair of waterproof boots, the small light, the beam drill, and the vial of dirt.

The objects made no sense to Qui-Gon. What did Lena have to know? And where had she been? Qui-Gon felt betrayed. She was not telling them the whole truth.

Although Lena appeared to be upset, Qui-Gon did not wait for her to calm down. "Where have you been?" he demanded.

Lena looked up, surprised by the stern tone of the Jedi's voice.

"Wandering," she replied. "I — I needed to be alone."

Qui-Gon was not satisfied. "Alone? Or just away from us?"

Lena's lip trembled and Qui-Gon noticed Obi-Wan was staring at him. He softened his tone slightly, but pressed on. "Why did you take the contents of the package with you?"

"That package is from Rutin," Lena said after a moment, struggling to control her voice. "He sent it to me before he . . ." She fought again for composure. "But how did he know he was going to die? And why didn't he tell me?"

Lena lost the struggle to suppress her frustrated grief and dropped her head into her hands. "He's trying to give me a message," she said after a moment, struggling to control her voice. "But I can't figure it out! It's as though he's speaking to me, and I can't hear him." Lena lost the struggle. . . . "He really is gone forever."

Mica and Obi-Wan rushed to join her on the couch, anxious to offer support. Qui-Gon stumbled back until he was sitting, facing the other three. Lena looked so much smaller than she had before. Less capable of deception, some-how.

Qui-Gon felt himself diminish as Lena's waves of grief washed into him, adding to the sea of sadness that never stopped pounding in his heart. Her words touched him deeply, and he had no more doubts about her sincerity. He, too, knew how the fact of a loved one's absence could strike with as savage a blow as the first realization. He knew that moment when the future ahead seemed empty and impossible to bear.

"The loved ones we have lost are always with us," Qui-Gon said. He was surprised to hear himself speaking, and surprised by his words. But they rendered comfort. Suddenly, it did feel as if Tahl were nearby, and the storm inside of him quieted a little.

There was a moment of thoughtful silence in the room. Obi-Wan gazed at his Master, his eyes full of compassion. And for the first time Qui-Gon did not feel the need to look away.

Lena's grief seemed to lift, and she looked at the Jedi Master gratefully. "It's true," she said, nodding. "Rutin is looking after me even now. He must have sent this package some time ago and arranged to have it delivered today. I'm sure it is meant to help me find evidence. He must have known that any information on the computer would be a target. He knew I would need something more."

Qui-Gon noticed that Mica paled as Lena spoke of the computer. He wondered if she was embarrassed that her plan hadn't worked, or frightened by the possibility that more evidence existed.

The young widow took no notice of her cousin. Her tears had stopped and the familiar strength was returning. Lena gathered the boots from the table and held them in her lap. "I haven't figured out the clue yet, but I will," she said firmly.

"Just please don't rush off like that again," Mica told her. "You scared me to death. We searched the park for hours."

Lena frowned. "The park . . ." she murmured.

Obi-Wan stared at the strange items on the table, then suddenly spoke. "Rutin had the package delivered to you here. So, he must have known about the hideout."

"Of course," Lena said. "Rutin was the one who secured this place. He was planning to hide here himself while he waited to be smuggled off the planet."

Suddenly, Lena leaped to her feet, knocking

the boots aside. "I almost forgot," she cried, pulling a datapad from her pocket. "While I was out I went by my apartment to see if I'd received a message from Zanita. She sent this."

CHAPTER 13

The sky outside the warehouse had darkened to a milky gray. Qui-Gon peered around the portal screens that masked the people inside from the streets below. It was getting late and the alleys were deserted.

"Meeting with Zanita is an unnecessary risk," Qui-Gon stated as he left the portal and paced the floor. He suddenly felt that leaving the planet as soon as possible was the best course of action. "We have the clues from Rutin, and should work with that. We do not need to place you or your mother-in-law in further danger."

"She's taking a risk because I asked her to," Lena argued. "I can't just let her wait in vain."

With a frown, Qui-Gon looked at the message on the datapad again.

TRANSPORT LOADING STATION, DOCK 12
10 P.M. TONIGHT
ALONE
FOR RUTIN

"I never should have gotten Zanita involved," Lena lamented. "But it is too late to change that now. If I can go alone, I can talk to her and convince her that I've changed my mind. I'll tell her I'm scared and have decided to leave the planet. Then we will all be safer."

Qui-Gon had to admit that it was not a bad plan. It would buy them some time and could even help them get off planet easier. He nodded his assent.

"But we won't let you go alone," Obi-Wan said. Mica looked relieved to hear this.

"Of course not," Qui-Gon echoed. "It is not safe."

"It is the only way I can convince Zanita," Lena argued. "She saw you at the estate. Surely she knows you are here representing the Galactic Republic. I will not be able to convince her I've changed my mind if she sees I am accompanied by Jedi!"

"We are here for your protection," Qui-Gon said firmly. *And to make sure you are what you say you are.* Learning that Lena had returned to her apartment when she was alone had once again aroused Qui-Gon's suspicions. She could have done any number of things while she was there. Though he accepted the sincerity of her grief, he would not lose sight of the fact that there could be pressures on her that he knew nothing about.

"I'm afraid you're stuck with us until we all arrive safely back on Coruscant." Obi-Wan smiled. "We will remain hidden, but we will not allow you to go alone."

Lena returned Obi-Wan's smile. "All right," she said. "We'd better hurry so we are first to arrive. It's not very far."

"Be careful," Mica said, embracing her cousin. "I'll be here if you need me. I'll *always* be here if you need me."

Lena touched her cousin's cheek. "I'll be right back!" she promised.

Qui-Gon, Obi-Wan, and Lena left the warehouse and made their way through the dark streets, lit only by the occasional light of the planet's two moons. Now that daylight had faded, Frego seemed a less inviting place. It was as though the darkness brought out the lies and deceit that pervaded the planet.

As the three neared the station, Qui-Gon and Obi-Wan fell back into the shadows. Lena insisted on walking boldly in the middle of the street, under the glowing lights.

"She should be more careful," Obi-Wan muttered.

"No, Padawan," Qui-Gon said. "She should not appear as if she has anything to hide. Besides, her presence will help to diminish ours."

Dock 12 was eerily silent. Low buildings rimmed a giant landing pad where huge transport ships were loaded with goods. The edges of the pad were almost completely dark.

Obi-Wan motioned to his Master and both Jedi leaped noiselessly onto a low rooftop. After making his way to the edge, Qui-Gon lay down next to Obi-Wan and the two watched Lena walk slowly into the orange square of light in the center of the landing pad. From their perch the Jedi could see everything, and they could be at Lena's side in a moment.

Although Lena's was the only shape Qui-Gon could make out in the darkness, he sensed they were not alone. He had felt another presence almost from the moment they had left the hideout, but now the feeling was stronger, more threatening.

From the opposite side of the pad, Zanita stepped into view. Lena moved with both arms out to greet her mother-in-law.

But Zanita did not raise her arms or offer any

greeting. After taking one more lurching step forward, the reason became clear.

Zanita's mouth was covered with a gag, and behind her, holding her bound arms firmly pressed against her back, was her oldest son, Solan Cobral.

CHAPTER 14

Obi-Wan leaped to his feet as three more figures emerged behind Solan and Zanita. But Qui-Gon pulled him back down.

Obi-Wan wrestled his arm free of his Master. He had to protect Lena. She was unarmed facing two droids, Solan Cobral, and his brother, Bard. The young widow was no match for men evil enough to hold their own mother captive, or order the death of their own brother.

"Not yet," Qui-Gon said softly. "I'd like to see what these men have in mind."

Obi-Wan sank to his knees. He would wait, for now. But if anyone made a move toward Lena, not even Qui-Gon would be able to stop him.

In the orange light of the landing pad Lena took a few steps back.

"Solan," she said. Her voice sounded strange to Obi-Wan, almost full of guilt. He wondered if she felt responsible for what was happening to Zanita.

"You were supposed to come alone," the crime boss boomed.

"I did," Lena replied without flinching.

Nervous that they had been spotted, Obi-Wan felt for his lightsaber. He tried to rise but Qui-Gon's hand on his shoulder pushed him back to his knees.

"Not us," Qui-Gon whispered.

"Don't hurt her," a voice cried in the darkness below. "She didn't know I was coming." Obi-Wan recognized the voice immediately. It was Mica. A moment later she was standing beside her cousin. Obi-Wan had not known she was there.

"Please, don't hurt Lena. She would never turn against the Cobral. She's only been trying to cover for me. I am the one you want. I am the one who knows how you operate. I am the one who wanted to testify against you."

"Mica, no. Be quiet," Lena whispered in an attempt to stop her cousin's outburst.

"Don't listen to her," Lena told the Cobrals. "She is protecting me. She doesn't know that I came tonight to tell Zanita I've changed my mind. I was a fool to think I could go against the Cobral. Solan, please hear me. You and Bard and Zanita are all I have left of my precious husband, Rutin. I realize that I need to hold on to the family I have, now more than ever. Where will I be if I drive you away? No matter what has happened in the past, we will always be family. And family is more important to me than anything."

"How wise," Solan replied, chuckling. He shoved Zanita toward Bard, who caught her with one hand. He held a blaster in the other.

"I'm touched that you still want to be a part of the family," he continued, taking a step closer. "And I'm grateful that you came together," he continued, walking closer still. "It will make cleaning up the mess you've made that much easier."

Solan dived toward Lena and Mica as the two droids closed in on either side.

Up on the roof, Obi-Wan knew it was time. Qui-Gon was at his side as he leaped off the roof and sprinted toward the helpless cousins.

Mica was caught in Solan's grasp, but Lena pulled away just in time. She turned to run and found herself face-to-face with a lanky but potentially lethal droid.

The one-eyed droid's arms shot out from its sides and began to wrap themselves around her. Lena ducked at the same moment Obi-Wan's lightsaber blade severed one arm, and with a mighty backswing separated the droid's head from its body.

Obi-Wan pushed Lena behind him and rushed to meet the other droid.

Beside him, Qui-Gon deflected a bolt from Bard's blaster, sending it toward Solan's feet. Solan struggled to hold on to Mica and train his blaster on the Jedi. He did not notice Lena sneaking up behind him.

Lena grabbed Solan's blaster. Mica whipped her body back and forth, delivering a sharp blow with her elbow to Solan's jaw. He lost his grip on both Mica and the weapon.

The second droid fired rapid bolts at Obi-Wan, who deflected them easily. Though the bolts turned and rained back on the droid, it did not show any damage. It continued to spray the pad with fire while rapidly extending a long arm to grab Mica.

Qui-Gon dispatched the arm with an elegant sweep of his lightsaber and stepped forward to finish the job. A slashing blow to the machine's midsection finally brought the droid down.

While Qui-Gon took care of the droid, Obi-Wan quickly surveyed the scene. Behind him Mica appeared to be in shock. She lay on the ground, staring into the darkness. Lena bravely held her blaster on Solan.

Suddenly, Obi-Wan leaped high in the air over Lena's head. He knew what was going to happen before it happened, but still was not in time to deflect the blast. From his spot deep in the shadows, still holding the bound-and-gagged Zanita, Bard fired his blaster straight at Lena.

Mica dived. Lena screamed. And the bolt found flesh.

CHAPTER 15

While Obi-Wan hurried toward the two women, Qui-Gon hit the ground running. He rushed toward Bard and his hostage, but could not see where they had gone in the darkness. He could merely hear the muffled sounds of the footsteps fleeing ahead of him.

Qui-Gon raced behind a building in time to see Solan climb into a repulsorlift vehicle. Bard shoved his mother in behind his brother, and the engine gunned.

Qui-Gon stopped short, his breath catching in his throat. The Cobrals had a vehicle waiting. It was useless to pursue them on foot. Besides, Qui-Gon was anxious to return to the dock. He had a terrible feeling about what he would find there.

Qui-Gon rounded the corner of the building. In the orange square of light he saw two figures kneeling. A third figure lay in his Padawan's arms. There was no life emanating from the body.

Mica was dead.

Lena threw herself onto her cousin's body, sobbing. "No, Mica," she cried, begging. "Not you. Don't leave me."

Qui-Gon stared at the scene before him, frozen. His mind flashed back to Tahl's last words to him. A horrible ache clenched his chest.

"Wherever I am headed, I will wait for you, Qui-Gon," she had said. "I've always been a solitary traveler."

"Not anymore," Qui-Gon had teased. "We will go on together. You promised, and you can't back out now. I'll never let you forget it."

Tahl had smiled slightly, and the effort drained her. Qui-Gon had known then that she was in grave danger. That she was going to die. He'd called on the Force, on the Jedi, on his great love for her. Nothing had been able to save the woman he loved.

Qui-Gon had rested his forehead against Tahl's. Their breath mingled. "Let my last moment be this one," she had said.

And it was.

"Master," Obi-Wan said quietly, and Qui-Gon was suddenly brought back to the moment. Lena was crumpled over Mica in front of him, wallowing in her pain. There was no trace of the strong, resolved woman Qui-Gon had met when he arrived on Frego. He did not see the woman who he thought might be deceiving them. He only saw a woman bent over a dead body, unable to cope with her agony.

He knew exactly how that felt. But he had survived, had gone on. And he believed that Lena could as well.

Qui-Gon bent down next to Lena. "I am so sorry," he said softly. "I know I cannot share your pain. But I do understand it."

With a shudder, Lena let go of Mica's body. "I would like to wrap the body," she said, wiping her eyes. "It is the custom here."

Obi-Wan found an old tarp outside a nearby ship, and Lena showed the Jedi the traditional way to enclose the body in it.

"Mica always looked out for me," Lena said as she lay the wrapped body gently on the ground. "She always tried to guide me in the right direction."

The three stood quietly together for a moment, silently saying good-bye. Then they left Mica lying in the pool of orange light.

"The park," Lena said as they slowly moved away from the body. "Mica said you'd searched it for hours."

"We did," Obi-Wan confirmed.

Lena's shoulders straightened and her eyes cleared. "I know what Rutin was trying to tell me," she said with sudden certainty. "We have to get to the park immediately."

Qui-Gon was amazed at Lena's ability to change her focus back to finding the necessary evidence. Her face was full of deep sadness, but she carried herself upright as she led them to the Tubal Park.

Once inside, Lena headed directly for a spot at the rear of the park. It was still dark, but the sky had completely cleared and the planet's two moons shone in the night sky. Their silver light partly lit the paths, bridges, and brooks.

Qui-Gon continuously scanned the area around them. He did not sense anything dangerous — the park seemed serene and peaceful, just as it had during the day. But it would have been foolish to let his guard down. Obi-Wan stood a distance away, alert for any trespass.

Suddenly, Lena stopped short next to a small stand of lush tropical trees. A stream gurgled over smooth rocks and into a pool of clear water.

With a sigh, Lena sat down. "This was our special place," she said. "I remember the first time Rutin brought me here four years ago. We were not even married yet. But we had so many plans, so many dreams." Her eyes shone with happiness for a brief moment. But before long, tears were welling in them and she broke down, sobbing.

"I'm so sorry," she said. "Sometimes it is more than I can bear. I find myself wishing that it was I who had been killed, not him. I would have gladly given my life to save his."

Qui-Gon nodded. "I, too, have wished I could have given my life to save another, one whom I had loved. But now I know that it is often harder to be the one left behind. I would not have wanted her to feel such loneliness, to go through the pain I have gone through." He touched Lena's arm briefly. "Rutin left these things for you because he knew his death was possible, and he trusted that you would carry on."

Qui-Gon looked into Lena's eyes, and knew that his words were getting through to her. Surprisingly, he felt a lightening in his own chest as well. His grief for Tahl was still excruciating, but he suddenly knew that there would come a time when it would be possible to bear. And in his heart he was certain that Tahl would want him to carry on, too. She would have hated the way he had chosen to mourn her, he realized suddenly. He had allowed his grief to remove him from everyone who had tried to help him. Because the weight of his sorrow was so terrible, he could not lift his head to see that others mourned her, too. Obi-Wan. Yoda. Bant. Clee Rhava. The list was long.

Her face rose in his mind. He could see the ironic twist to her lips.

"*Now* who's blind?" she said.

Her voice was so real to him. How he wished he could answer. . . .

"Thank you, Qui-Gon," Lena said softly, breaking his reverie. "As difficult as it is to live without Rutin, I know that you are right."

Qui-Gon briefly squeezed Lena's hand. He noticed that his Padawan's face wore a look of confused frustration, and felt he had some explaining to do. But now was not the time to discuss it. They had to find the evidence and leave the planet.

"Do you have any ideas about what the clues from the package mean?" Qui-Gon asked.

Lena got to her feet and began to look under rocks and thick green leaves. "I'm sure this is the spot," she explained. "But the clues don't make any sense to me. Why would I need a drill? Or a pair of boots?"

The three searched the area, finding nothing but grass, water, rocks, and plants.

"There's nothing here," Obi-Wan finally said,

sounding exasperated. "It's just like any other lovely spot in the woods."

Hearing his words, Lena suddenly looked up. "But it isn't, of course," she said. "It's all manufactured. Humanmade." She began to look at the ground in a new way. She stepped across a patch of fake ground covered with moss. Getting to her knees, she peeled it back.

Underneath was a large, locked panel.

Lena picked up the beam drill and forced the panel open. Lifting it aside, she found a short tunnel descending down.

Excited, Lena lowered herself into the tunnel. A moment later Qui-Gon heard a loud splash.

"Well, I know what the boots were for," she called up. "I'm up to my ankles in water. But at least it's not sewage!"

Qui-Gon handed Lena the boots. They were big, and Lena pulled them on over her shoes. Then she turned on the flashlight and splashed around. She was inside a small pump room.

"Do you need help?" Obi-Wan called down.

There was some more splashing, but no response. Then several moments of complete silence.

Qui-Gon and his Padawan exchanged glances. Qui-Gon was just about to lower himself into the tunnel when they heard a gleeful shout.

"I found it!" Lena exclaimed.

A moment later she emerged with a second small package in a waterproof sheathing.

Qui-Gon hoped it was the evidence they needed.

CHAPTER 16

The three wasted no time getting back to the warehouse. They had been at the park for a couple of hours, and it was now very early morning.

Obi-Wan was anxious to get to the makeshift apartment and open the package. He was also exhausted, and hoped they would be able to rest for a few hours before planning their next move. But then his Master was never one to rest. There had been many times when Obi-Wan was certain that the older Jedi simply did not need sleep.

Once safely inside the warehouse, Lena ripped open the package. Inside was a datapad, well wrapped and protected from water or shaking. Lena switched the tiny machine on and they all waited while it hummed to life.

The next few moments seemed to go on for

hours. Her hands a bit shaky, Lena put the data-pad on a low table and sat down on the sofa.

The datapad beeped.

Lena pressed a series of buttons on the side of the machine, and information began to flash across the screen. Information about illegal land negotiations, bribery, government extortion, contracts for murders . . . the list of crimes went on and on.

"Say good-bye to power, Solan," she whispered. Lena looked up at the Jedi, smiling. "This will put the Cobral behind bars for a long, long time," she said.

Obi-Wan sighed in relief. Soon this mission would be over. Lena would be safe, and Frego would be free.

Qui-Gon did not waste any time in contacting Senator Crote on Coruscant. He explained that they had the evidence they needed, and they would be traveling with it first thing in the morning.

"Wonderful," the senator replied. "Take the *Degarian II*. It is fast and available. I look forward to seeing you tomorrow."

With nothing more to do, Lena and the Jedi settled down for a few hours' rest. But while Lena slept in the room next door and his Master dozed nearby, Obi-Wan found that, exhausted as he was, sleep evaded him. He kept remem-

bering the conversation he'd overheard between his Master and Lena in the park. Qui-Gon
had never spoken so frankly about his grief —
to anyone. Why did he choose to confide in a
woman he barely trusted, and not in his own
Padawan?

Obi-Wan knew that Tahl's death was incredi-
bly hard for Qui-Gon. He knew now that his
Master was in love with her. But while Tahl was
alive Obi-Wan had not fully recognized that
their love existed. When did it blossom? Qui-
Gon and Tahl barely had any time together that
he knew about.

As Obi-Wan lay in the darkness, guilt washed
over him. He knew it was not right for him to be
upset with his Master. Who he chose to confide
in was his decision. And if it was not Obi-Wan,
so be it.

Rolling over, Obi-Wan remembered his
Master's words to Lena. He remembered the
look in Qui-Gon's eyes. And more than anything, he wished he could find a way to ease his
Master's pain.

At last the fatigue of the mission overcame
Obi-Wan and he began to drift into sleep. But
just as his senses were falling into a more
relaxed state, he heard movement in Lena's
room.

Obi-Wan sat up, wondering for half a moment if Lena was trying to escape without them — if his Master had been right to question her motives all along. She'd spoken convincingly to Solan, perhaps she really did want to make amends with the Cobral. Then Obi-Wan heard a second set of footsteps and a struggle. Someone was attacking Lena!

Checking to make sure his lightsaber was safely at his side, Obi-Wan broke into Lena's room. Lena sat on a chair, bound and gagged. A figure wearing a hooded burgundy tunic stood over her.

Launching himself into the air, Obi-Wan somersaulted over the two of them, pulling back the figure's hood. He expected to find the face of a Cobral, but did not recognize the stranger, whose face contorted into a tangle of rage as he drew a blaster.

Obi-Wan was ready with his lightsaber, but the intruder quickly shoved something into his pocket and made for the transparisteel portal. He was about to disappear when Qui-Gon burst into the room and knocked the man into the wall with a Force wave. The intruder slid to the floor and was still.

Obi-Wan quickly untied Lena. "Are you all right?" he asked.

Lena nodded. "Another thug working for the

Cobral," she said, cracking a half smile. "I'm almost getting used to them."

"Good timing, Master," Obi-Wan said wryly as he helped Lena to her feet.

"Thank you," Qui-Gon replied as he bent over the man. "He's going to wake up with quite a headache, I'm afraid."

Qui-Gon had not cracked a joke in weeks, and it was music to Obi-Wan's ears.

Qui-Gon searched the man's pockets and quickly retrieved Rutin's datapad. He retrieved something else, Obi-Wan saw, but concealed it in his hand.

Qui-Gon stood up and faced Lena and Obi-Wan. His face was grave with concern.

"There's been a change in plans. We must leave Frego as soon as possible," he said.

CHAPTER 17

Lena, Qui-Gon, and Obi-Wan were silent as they once again made their way through the darkened streets of Rian. It was almost dawn, and a pale yellow light was beginning to overtake the sky. Qui-Gon was anxious for the mission to be over. But as he strode purposefully ahead, he could not shake the feeling that they were far from the end.

When they arrived at one of the city's many landing platforms, Obi-Wan headed straight for the *Degarian II.* He was practically boarding the ship before Qui-Gon was able to catch up to him. Lena was at his heels.

"No, Padawan," Qui-Gon said quietly, pulling him aside. "We will not be taking this ship." Qui-Gon gestured with his head toward a lone vehicle in the corner of the launch bay. "I believe that this one will better serve our purposes."

Obi-Wan looked momentarily confused, then

he nodded. He gently steered Lena away from the *Degarian II* and guided her to a shadowy area of the platform.

Qui-Gon approached the pilot of the smaller ship. "We're looking for passage to Coruscant," he explained in a low voice. "We'd like to leave as soon as possible."

The pilot stopped what he was doing and stood to his full height, which was considerable. He did not say anything at first, but simply looked Qui-Gon in the eye. Qui-Gon returned his gaze without flinching. He felt confident that this man was not in league with the Cobral. Flying with him would be relatively safe.

"I can fly you to Coruscant," the pilot finally said. He named his fee, which seemed a fair price.

Qui-Gon agreed. "We have some business to attend to, but will return shortly," he said.

The pilot nodded. "I will be ready."

Qui-Gon turned and headed back to Obi-Wan and Lena. Now he only had to make it appear as if they were leaving the planet on the *Degarian II*, as planned.

"Time to board," he said in a normal voice as he walked up the boarding ramp. Then he quietly added to Obi-Wan, "Let me do the talking."

The *Degarian II* was a large and comfortable ship, with a diplomatic lounge and roomy sleeping quarters for its passengers. The Jedi and Lena were greeted by a droid host as soon as they got on board.

Qui-Gon was surprised to see that the droid was identical to those he and Obi-Wan had cut down earlier in the evening, but greeted the droid as if he were expecting him. After chatting for a few brief moments and accepting a message of welcome from Senator Crote, Qui-Gon declared that they were all very tired and would like to retire to their resting quarters.

"That will be fine," the droid replied. "I can show you the way." It led them down a long hall to a trio of spacious rooms.

"Thank you," Qui-Gon said. "Please be sure to wake us before we arrive."

The droid nodded. "Of course. We have clearance to leave in twenty minutes." He stood for a moment, as if waiting to make sure that each of them went into a room. Lena yawned and said good night, then disappeared through a doorway. Obi-Wan did the same, and Qui-Gon followed.

Qui-Gon waited for a good fifteen minutes before knocking on Lena's door.

"We're getting off early," Qui-Gon said as Obi-Wan appeared behind him.

Lena looked confused. "Do you think it is safe?" she asked.

"Safer than staying on board," Obi-Wan replied with a grimace.

Qui-Gon started down the hall and the others followed closely behind. They escaped through a small hatch at the back of the ship just as the craft's engines hummed to life. They were boarding the other ship by the time the *Degarian II* disappeared into the atmosphere above them.

As soon as everyone was safely on board, Qui-Gon explained what had just transpired. "I'm afraid Senator Crote is not what he appears to be." He pulled a travel order bearing the official Fregan senatorial seal from his pocket. It also bore Senator Crote's signature. "I found this on the thug who tried to steal Rutin's evidence."

Lena's eyes widened. "The senator?" she exclaimed. "I felt certain he was above this — that he was not part of the corruption."

"I have felt certain of many things that have not been so," Qui-Gon replied. "There are many hidden truths in a galaxy such as ours."

Lena sat back and rubbed her eyes. She was clearly overwhelmed. It seemed there was no end to the Cobral web of lies.

"Obviously I did not think it worth the risk to fly on the *Degarian II*," Qui-Gon continued. He flashed a brief smile. "I think we've taken enough risks already."

The small vessel took off a short while later, and the Jedi and Lena settled in for the journey. Though the ship was not nearly as large or as fancy as the *Degarian II*, Qui-Gon noticed that a sense of calm came over the group as they rose into the air. They were finally leaving Frego behind.

When the ship was about halfway to Coruscant, Qui-Gon was startled out of his meditative state by the buzz of his comlink. A moment later Yoda's familiar voice began to speak.

"Been attacked the *Degarian II* has," he said simply. His statement was followed by a few seconds of silence. Then, "Survivors there are not."

CHAPTER 18

Jedi Master Mace Windu met Qui-Gon, Obi-Wan, and Lena at the landing platform. It had been a long journey, and it was afternoon on the city-planet of Coruscant. The sun was high in the sky, making reflections on the thousands of on-planet transport vehicles and glinting off of the towering skyscrapers.

"You must be Lena Cobral," Master Windu said, taking her hand for a moment. "It is good to finally meet you."

He looked at each of them in turn before leading them into the Jedi Temple. "We are grateful that you are safe," he said. "The news of Senator Crote came as a surprise, and obviously not a pleasant one. Then when the *Degarian II* was destroyed . . ."

Obi-Wan winced as he remembered how close they had all come to being killed. "We would like to get Lena on the stand as soon as possible," he said, changing the subject.

"Of course," Mace agreed. "The chancellor has called a special hearing for this afternoon. It is scheduled to start in just a few hours. The entire senate will be present."

"Excellent," Qui-Gon said. "We do not want to give Senator Crote or the Cobral time to realize that their plan has failed — that we are all still very much alive." He briefly touched Lena's shoulder. "And we can take care of this matter once and for all. It is best for Frego, I think."

Lena nodded. "In the meantime I'd like to freshen up and change my clothes." She gestured to her dirty travel clothing. "I fear this is not appropriate for a special session of the Galactic Senate."

Obi-Wan smiled. Even under extreme pressure, Lena attended to details. He would miss her when their mission was over, he realized. And it would be over very soon.

"We have readied some chambers in the Fregan consulate for you," Mace said. "We believe that Senator Crote will be out of the building until the hearing. But if we run into him we must all behave as though we have not linked him to the Cobral in any way."

"I understand," Lena said. "But I hope you

are right when you say he is out of the building."

Mace led the way to Lena's temporary quarters and the Jedi waited while she quickly freshened up and changed her clothes.

Obi-Wan was amazed when she reemerged a few minutes later. Her hair had been tied into an elaborate twist, and a pair of sparkling gem earrings dangled from her earlobes. A simple light blue gown hung just to her ankles. She looked lovely and not at all like she had been through a long, harrowing night.

The group left the consulate and went directly to the Senate.

Lena gasped when she entered the Senate chamber. "I had no idea the galaxy was so big!" she whispered to Obi-Wan nervously.

Obi-Wan gave her a reassuring smile. "You'll be fine," he whispered back. "Remember, you are doing what is right."

Lena squared her shoulders and nodded as the group took their place on the large floating platform. She took her seat as the platform smoothly glided toward the front of the giant chamber. The session was just beginning, and Senators from all over the galaxy were craning their heads to see who would be speaking at this special meeting.

After a few minutes the murmur echoing throughout the room began to die down. Chancellor Valorum signaled to Lena that it was time for her to speak.

Steadying herself on her chair, she got to her feet. For a moment she was silent as she looked out at the thousands of faces staring back at her. Obi-Wan could only guess at what was running through her mind. She had been through so much, come so far. Now her fate was in the hands of strangers. Would they believe her? Would they care?

Lena's voice did not wobble as she spoke out about the Cobral. When she linked the crime family to Senator Crote there was a murmur in the chamber followed by respectful silence. Obi-Wan could tell Lena had the attention of every being in the room as she spoke of crimes, abused power, and the evil Cobral hold on Frego. Then she told her own story, including the death of her husband and cousin. And finally Senator Crote's attempt to have them all killed.

There was an uproar in the chamber as a stunned Senator Crote leaped to his feet. "You are lying!" he shouted. "I have done nothing but good for your planet!"

But Obi-Wan could tell by the look on the senator's face that the man knew the tide was against him as Lena presented the proof — not only his link to the thug who had attacked her, but transmissions that linked him definitively with the destruction of the *Degarian II*. His political career — and in fact his life as a free man — was over.

It did not take long to tally the vote. Senator Crote was removed from office, and the Cobral were immediately ordered under arrest, to be tried for their crimes. Once a new government was in place, a new senator of Frego would be elected.

Obi-Wan beamed. He was so proud of Lena, of all that she had accomplished for her planet and her people.

Because of her, Frego would finally get its new beginning, its chance at a new life.

CHAPTER 19

Back at the Fregan consulate, a small party was going on in Lena's chambers. There was much talk of the success of the testimony and the new road ahead. A few senators were so impressed by Lena's testimony that they suggested she run for the Fregan senatorial position.

"I have no interest in such a position," she replied flatly. "I will return to Frego to help put the transition government in place. But afterward it will be time for me to start a new life on a new planet."

She winked at Obi-Wan, and he had a feeling that politics were definitely in Lena's future. Perhaps she would get a position as an aide of some sort on Coruscant. If she did, he realized, he might get to see her from time to time. . . .

After the small group had shared a celebratory meal together, Lena announced that she wanted to get some rest. "So much has happened, and I'd like a little time to digest it all. Soon enough I'll be heading back to Frego. I'm afraid I won't be getting much rest there."

Qui-Gon nodded. He knew how much work it was to change governments. "I certainly think a rest is in order," he said. "Jedi Master Mace Windu and I have Temple business to attend to, but I will be back shortly. Obi-Wan can stay with you, if you like."

"That's very kind, but I'd really like some time alone," Lena replied graciously.

Obi-Wan tried to hide his disappointment as he nodded. "Of course," he said.

While Mace and Qui-Gon left for the Temple, Obi-Wan lingered outside Lena's door. He wanted to respect her wishes, but also wanted to stay close by in case she changed her mind. The door to the adjacent chamber was open and the room was empty. Obi-Wan entered and sat down in a comfortable chair. From here he could hear what was going on in Lena's room.

Obi-Wan had just closed his eyes when he heard a familiar voice. It was not Lena's, and it was not friendly.

"Surprised to see me, Lena dear?" it said. "I suppose you would be. But then I thought you loved surprises."

There was a muffled sound, as if the intruder

was fiddling with some clothing. Then Obi-Wan heard Lena gasp.

Obi-Wan was out in the hallway in less than a second. With his hand on his lightsaber, he pressed the door controls. But nothing happened. The door was jammed.

Obi-Wan ignited his lightsaber. He'd have to cut through the door. But as his blade touched the entrance, something told him not to cut.

Concentrating, he closed his eyes. He heard a very slight scraping right in front of him. Lena was just centimeters away — on the other side of the door. There was no way for him to cut through without putting her at risk.

"I should have done this years ago," the intruder continued. "Perhaps then I could have saved my favorite son. The one I loved the most. The one I cherished."

Zanita.

"I tried to save him, I really did. But once word got out that he wanted to betray the family — that you had talked him into testifying against his own flesh and blood, there was nothing I could do. It was a great loss for me, yes. But necessary."

Lena let go of a sob. "Necessary?" she echoed in disbelief. "Zanita, he was your own son!"

"I know that, Lena. Actually, I rather wished

he had been a daughter. You see, boys and men are nothing but foolish pawns. They always need to be told what to do, and half the time they still do it wrong. Things on Frego were a mess until I took control. I organized our forces and got the government to see matters our way. Everything was going just fine until you came along. You stole my Rutin's heart and coerced his mind."

"Rutin had a mind of his own," Lena said quietly.

Scanning the wall, Obi-Wan tried to remember the position of everything inside the quarters. His hands were damp with sweat, and his heart was pounding. He didn't have much time to act, or any room for error.

Zanita acted as if she didn't hear her daughter-in-law. "And now because of you I stand to lose my other two sons as well," she went on. "But of course I'm not going to let that happen."

Obi-Wan heard an ominous click. He had to act — he just hoped he wasn't already too late. Raising his lightsaber, he pushed the blade into the wall.

"Would you like a moment to fix your hair, darling?" Zanita asked. "You might be seeing Rutin in a few moments."

Obi-Wan sliced through the wall with remarkable speed — and stepped inside just in time to see Lena fall to the floor, meters away. She landed with a sickening thud and lay completely still.

Still holding a blaster in her hand, Zanita leveled the barrel at her daughter-in-law's chest. She did not seem to be aware of Obi-Wan's presence.

Obi-Wan tore his eyes away from Lena and took several steps toward Zanita. She whirled around suddenly, the blaster now aimed at him.

"Ah, a Jedi," she said. "Of course."

She fired several rapid blasts. Obi-Wan was surprised by her incredible accuracy, and had to dodge and weave to avoid being hit by two and deflect three of the bolts with his saber at the same time.

Stepping forward, he felt one of the bolts graze his robe. He spun around and leaped into the air, landing on Zanita's right side and grabbing the blaster. Zanita hurled herself forward onto Lena's body. Her shoulders shook violently as several sobs escaped her throat.

The true leader of the Cobral had been defeated, and was probably thinking of the time she would soon be spending in prison.

Obi-Wan deactivated his lightsaber and reclipped it to his belt. There was a small hole in his robe where the blaster bolt had grazed him.

He fingered it gingerly, grateful that he was not wounded. But Lena . . .

All of a sudden Obi-Wan heard a rushing sound behind him.

"Obi-Wan, look out!" someone shouted. It was Qui-Gon.

For a split second Obi-Wan was not sure where to look. Then he saw the glimmer of a weapon in Zanita's hand. It was a vibroblade.

Before Obi-Wan could disarm her a second time, Zanita had plunged the reverberating blade into her chest.

A moment later she fell to the floor next to Lena, dead.

Qui-Gon looked up from his sleep couch in his quarters at the Jedi Temple to see his Padawan standing in the doorway.

"I thought you might like to come with me to see Lena," he explained.

Obi-Wan shifted his feet slightly, and Qui-Gon was reminded of the young boy he had taken as a Padawan learner more than four years before. Impatient and headstrong, but also unsure. They had come a long way since then. But at that moment Qui-Gon was very aware that the younger Jedi still sought his affection and approval. Qui-Gon could not blame him, and was even grateful. Soon enough Obi-Wan would be a Jedi Knight in his own right, and would no longer need him. For the moment, however, he was still a boy.

Things between them had not been very smooth of late, Qui-Gon knew. He felt a twinge of guilt. He was not sure why it was so difficult for him to confide in the boy when it came to his feelings. Like many things, it simply was.

"I would like that," Qui-Gon said, getting to his feet. "How is she doing?"

"The blow to her head when she fell was quite severe," Obi-Wan replied. "But she is recovering well and is set to be released this afternoon. She is planning to return to Frego the day after tomorrow."

Qui-Gon set his pace to match Obi-Wan's as they made their way down the corridor. "Physical wounds heal quickly," he said quietly. "It is the emotional ones that require more time."

Qui-Gon was silent as they made their way down the hall. Then he spoke. "When Tahl died, the wound was so broad and so deep that I was certain I could not live. I could not go on. And in my pain I was blind to those around me — those who also loved and mourned Tahl."

"I grieved her as well," Obi-Wan said. "But I knew that my grief did not match yours, that it never would. I did not know how to help you. I was lost."

Suddenly Qui-Gon stopped and turned to face his Padawan. "I am the one who was lost, Padawan. You were generous and patient with me. And I needed that patience. I still carry the wound I suffered when I lost Tahl. I will for the rest of my life."

Obi-Wan nodded solemnly. "I know," he said softly.

Qui-Gon placed a hand on Obi-Wan's shoulder. "I am grateful for your efforts to help me through my pain. For a long time I was not ready to hear your words, but you were still right to speak them. Thanks to you I have found myself again — I have found a way to go on. Your words . . . *you* are a comfort to me. Thank you."

Obi-Wan let out a deep breath and smiled. "You're welcome," he said.

Visit **www.scholastic.com/starwars**
and discover

The Early Adventures of
Obi-Wan Kenobi and Qui-Gon Jinn

JEDI APPRENTICE

☐ BDN 0-590-51922-0	#1: The Rising Force	$4.99 US
☐ BDN 0-590-51925-5	#2: The Dark Rival	$4.99 US
☐ BDN 0-590-51933-6	#3: The Hidden Past	$4.99 US
☐ BDN 0-590-51934-4	#4: The Mark of the Crown	$4.99 US
☐ BDN 0-590-51956-5	#5: The Defenders of the Dead	$4.99 US
☐ BDN 0-590-51969-7	#6: The Uncertain Path	$4.99 US
☐ BDN 0-590-51970-0	#7: The Captive Temple	$4.99 US
☐ BDN 0-590-52079-2	#8: The Day of Reckoning	$4.99 US
☐ BDN 0-590-52080-6	#9: The Fight for Truth	$4.99 US
☐ BDN 0-590-52084-9	#10: The Shattered Peace	$4.99 US
☐ BDN 0-439-13930-9	#11: The Deadly Hunter	$4.99 US
☐ BDN 0-439-13931-7	#12: The Evil Experiment	$4.99 US
☐ BDN 0-439-13932-5	#13: The Dangerous Rescue	$4.99 US
☐ BDN 0-439-13933-3	#14: The Ties That Bind	$4.99 US
☐ BDN 0-439-13934-1	#15: The Death of Hope	$4.99 US
☐ BDN 0-439-13935-X	#16: The Call to Vengeance	$4.99 US

Also available:

☐ BDN 0-590-52093-8	*Star Wars* Journal: Episode I: Anakin Skywalker	$5.99 US
☐ BDN 0-590-52101-2	*Star Wars* Journal: Episode I: Queen Amidala	$5.99 US
☐ BDN 0-439-13941-4	*Star Wars* Journal: Episode I: Darth Maul	$5.99 US
☐ BDN 0-590-01089-1	*Star Wars*: Episode I— The Phantom Menace	$5.99 US

Scholastic Inc., P.O. Box 7502, Jefferson City, MO 65102

Please send me the books I have checked above. I am enclosing $_____ (please add $2.00 to cover shipping and handling). Send check or money order–no cash or C.O.D.s please.

Name_____ Birthdate_____

Address_____

City_____ State/Zip_____

Please allow four to six weeks for delivery. Offer good in U.S.A. only. Sorry, mail orders are not available to residents of Canada. Prices subject to change.

SWA1201